She watched him

Quint McCabe brushed the brim of his battered hat before going to collect his saddle and bridle. He carried them to the corral, where he draped the bridle over a post, swung the saddle over the top rail, then started to inspect it.

He'd certainly left Katlin with no doubt that, in his eyes, she was a nuisance. Her purpose would be well served, though, if she had to prove herself to him. Because once she showed him she wouldn't cause any problems, she could work on winning his trust.

And she had to win his trust—even if she didn't deserve it. She didn't want to become interested in the way a ranch operated. She didn't care about the life of a modern-day cowboy. She was here for one reason— to learn just what had happened during her brother's last mission.

ABOUT THE AUTHOR

Although Ginger Chambers currently resides outside Texas, from accent to attitude she's still a proud product of the Lone Star State. "Writing a book set in Texas is almost as good as being there," she says. "And the Parkers of West Texas have become family. I love each and every character." Check Ginger's web page at www.superauthors.com for information on her next book about the West Texans, coming soon from Harlequin Superromance.

HIDDEN IN TEXAS
Ginger Chambers

HARLEQUIN®

TORONTO • NEW YORK • LONDON
AMSTERDAM • PARIS • SYDNEY • HAMBURG
STOCKHOLM • ATHENS • TOKYO • MILAN • MADRID
PRAGUE • WARSAW • BUDAPEST • AUCKLAND

ISBN 0-373-70907-2

HIDDEN IN TEXAS

Copyright © 2000 by Ginger Chambers.

This edition published by arrangement with Harlequin Books S.A.

® and TM are trademarks of the publisher. Trademarks indicated with
® are registered in the United States Patent and Trademark Office, the
Canadian Trade Marks Office and in other countries.

Visit us at www.eHarlequin.com

Printed in U.S.A.

HIDDEN IN TEXAS

CHAPTER ONE

QUINT MCCABE sat at the table in his aunt and uncle's kitchen enjoying the human contact afforded by one of his infrequent visits to ranch headquarters. That was...he'd been enjoying himself until his cousin, Morgan Hughes, disclosed what Mae Parker, the matriarch of the Parker family, had requested of him. Then his entire defense system went on alert.

"Now, Mae's *askin'*," Morgan summed up, "but we all know what *that* means."

Quint stared at his cousin, who'd inherited his blond hair and pale blue eyes from the same source as Quint—their maternal grandfather. "Why me?" he demanded.

"She says it's because she can trust you."

Quint grimaced, even as his aunt Delores said stoutly, "Well, I should think so!"

His uncle Dub frowned. "What in the name of heaven is Mae thinkin'? She'd'a never agreed to somethin' like this in her younger days. Not even a couple of years ago. Sendin' a woman out alone to stay with a single cowboy! No offense, son. Nothin' against you. But...I can't figure it out."

"Rafe's tried talkin' her out of it," Morgan said,

naming Mae Parker's great-nephew and the present head of operations at the Parker Ranch.

"So it's a done deal," Quint muttered grimly.

"Mae still wants to meet the woman, talk to her in person before givin' the final go-ahead. But if she passes muster, I'll be bringing her out your way early next week."

"How long is she planning to stay?" Quint asked.

"As long as she wants, I reckon. A week, maybe two? Probably what caught Mae's fancy is the subject matter. *The Vanishing Texas Cowboy*—that's the title of the magazine series the woman's gonna do."

Dub snorted derisively. "Ain't vanishin' as far as I can see." For most of his seventy-three years Dub had been the foreman of the Parker Ranch, a job he'd turned over to Morgan nine years earlier.

"Maybe that's what Mae wants to show her," Morgan's pretty brunette wife, Christine, said as she kept an eye on their active three-year-old playing in a sunbeam by the window.

"Then why not have her talk to the hands livin' at the bunkhouse?" Dub demanded. "Why send her out to a remote spot like Big Spur to bother Quint?"

"It seems the lady has requested it special," Morgan explained. "Says she wants to walk in the 'boot-prints' of a cowboy even other cowboys consider a loner. Someone who lives and works on his own. Who doesn't have contact with anyone for days, sometimes weeks, on end. She seems to think her readers will find that fascinatin'.''

Quint's taut muscles grew tighter. He'd found a place away from the world, away from prying eyes. He didn't want to have to deal with this magazine woman, or anyone else. Yet he was in no position to refuse. The Parkers had accepted him back on the ranch—even given him the assignment he'd most desired—when three years ago he'd returned to West Texas, suddenly out of a promising career in the military and close-lipped about the cause. Like the Hugheses, they must have suspected he'd committed a serious infraction. But that hadn't stopped them from welcoming him, just as they had when, at age fourteen, he'd been sent to live with his aunt and uncle while his father was on a difficult assignment. He'd taken naturally to ranch work, winning their respect during the three years he'd spent here.

''What, exactly, am I supposed to do with her?'' he asked. ''Give her lessons on tending cattle?''

''She wants to *watch* you,'' Morgan said dryly.

Dub snorted again, but before he could make another caustic observation, Quint asked, ''Does anyone know anything about her?''

''Just that she works for *Eyes On Texas* magazine,'' Morgan said.

Delores jumped up from the table to rifle through a batch of magazines stacked on a counter. ''You know, I think I have a copy of that. I put these aside to pass on to you, Christine. Here!'' She pulled a magazine free of the others. ''Here it is!''

All eyes fastened on the glossy cover. Beneath the boldly printed masthead was a picture of a pair of shiny new ostrich-skin cowboy boots with several coils of rope wrapped around them. At the spot where the rope left the boots and touched the hardscrabble ground, it transformed into a diamondback rattler—head up, ready to strike. Possibly to soften the threat, a jackrabbit peeked out from behind the snake, completely oblivious to any danger.

Quint frowned. ''What kind of magazine is it?''

''It has articles and interviews, tells about things happenin' around the state,'' Delores said. ''Kinda pokes fun at some people, too.''

''Fun with a sting,'' Christine added. ''Shannon has a subscription.'' She named Rafe Parker's wife.

''Shannon gave me this,'' Delores said, tapping the issue. ''I don't remember an article by a Katlin Carter, though…but at the time, I wasn't lookin'. That's her name, isn't it, Morgan? Katlin Carter?''

''That's it,'' Morgan said.

Christine scanned the table of contents. ''Nothing here by her that I see. Maybe she's not a regular contributor.''

Morgan's lips curled and his eyes twinkled, a sure sign that he was about to devil someone. ''What's up, Quint? You hopin' to find out if she's good-lookin'? Think it might help pass the time while she's out there with you?''

Dub immediately joined in. "Or could be...if she's *not* good-lookin', it'll be all that much easier for him *not* to be tempted!"

Quint took their ribbing good-naturedly. "I don't care *what* she looks like. If Mae wants me to baby-sit her, I guess I'll be doing it. The first part of next week you'll be coming, you say Morgan?"

"She has her meetin' with Mae this Tuesday."

"I'll stay close to camp."

"If we don't turn up by noon Wednesday, do whatever you want. You know how touchy Mae can be. If there's somethin' she doesn't like about this Katlin Carter, the woman won't stand two whoops in hell of gettin' her okay."

"I still think the ol' gal's startin' to lose it," Dub grumbled.

"You'd say that to her face, would you, Dad?"

"Hell no! I'd lose somethin' myself if I did!"

Quint joined in the ensuing laughter. The Hugheses were good people. They lived their lives simply and were as protective of the Parker Ranch as the Parkers themselves. A Hughes had lived and worked on the ranch, mostly at Little Springs—the foreman's home—for almost as long as there'd been a ranch. They were considered "family" long before Morgan's marriage to Christine, a Parker heir. Rafe and Morgan had grown up like brothers and were still just as close.

Quint had become steeped in ranch lore and history during his younger days here. Once he'd even had a major tussle inside himself about what to do with his life. Whether to follow through with his long-held plan to go into the Army like his father, or continue cowboying. In the end, his original plan had won out. Only now, here he was, back tending cattle.

He wrenched his mind away from uncomfortable thoughts and concentrated instead on what his aunt had asked him. He patted his flat stomach. "No, thanks, Aunt Delores, I'm stuffed. No room for dessert."

"I have to try to fatten you up," his aunt retorted, "otherwise, what would I tell Heddy when we talk? She's always askin' me how you are. I can't tell her that every time I see you—*when* you decide to come in—you look like the last time you had a good meal was the last time I saw you."

"I make myself good meals."

"Not as good as mine!"

Quint gazed at the abundant remains of their earlier lunch spread over table and counter. "Well, that's true," he conceded.

"Leave the boy alone, woman," Dub chided. "He's doin' all right. Hard work's good for a person. Better than this roll I'm sproutin' around my middle since I'm not up and out every mornin'. You see any extra fat on Morgan? He works it off, that's what he does. Just like I used to. Just like Quint does."

"I've made a couple of pound cakes I want you

to take along to Big Spur, Quint,'' Delores declared. ''And I won't take no for an answer.''

''I'll be happy to have 'em,'' Quint said, a smile flickering across his lips.

The women began to clear the table and the men filed onto the back porch. From there they moved into the shade of one of the area's few trees.

A hot summer breeze stirred the air, bringing with it the pungent smells of grasses and cattle.

''I still can't figure out what Mae's up to,'' Dub said, returning to their previous topic as he settled on an old wooden chair propped against the tree trunk.

Morgan hunkered down across from him, as did Quint.

''I don't even want to try,'' Morgan said, reaching for a spear of grass that he immediately started to worry. ''I learned a long time ago to stay out of the way when she's got a bee in her bonnet. You taught me that, Dad.''

''Wish *I* could stay out of her way,'' Quint remarked.

Morgan glanced at him. ''It's probably what she said. She knows she can trust you, and since you fit the bill in all the other ways, you're the one she picked.''

''You think she wants to bring attention to the ranch for some reason?'' Dub asked.

''Who knows?'' Morgan tossed the stripped grass stem away.

They contemplated the matter in silence for a time, before Dub asked Quint, "You doin' all right up in Big Spur? This year's calves seem to be gettin' on okay?"

"All that I've seen are doing fine."

"You remember to call your momma?"

"I called her."

Dub approved. "Good. That'll make her happy."

"Which'll make *Mom* happy…which, in turn, will make *Dad* happy." Morgan grinned. "Domestic tranquility in these parts always revolves around the little things, Quint. If you remember to call Aunt Heddy, the barn cats end up gettin' extra cream the next mornin'!"

Dub eyed his son. "I remember not too many years ago when we were waitin' on calls from you. Back before you and Christine got hitched. When you were off in the Panhandle chasin' rustlers for the Cattlemen's Association. There were times when those poor ol' cats didn't see cream from one week to the next. Your momma kept thinkin' you'd been shot. You'll see what it's like when one of yours takes it into her head to move off the ranch for a spell. It's not easy bein' a parent! That's why we set such store in hearin' from our kids when they're away, no matter how old they are. Your momma feels the same, Quint, even if she is used to the occasional separation, what with your dad and you havin' been in the service and—"

His uncle recognized the slip as soon as the words

left his mouth. Dub's jaw clamped shut; his ear tips turned bright pink. Out of respect for Quint's feelings, the family treated his time in the military—a good fourteen years from the day he'd joined at eighteen to when he'd…left at age thirty-two—as if it didn't exist. They never talked about it in his hearing, never even mentioned it.

Morgan did his best to salve the moment by imparting some seemingly forgotten information about the ranch. He talked about that for a time, before he and his dad moved on to other things.

After a bit, Quint stood up. Everything inside him was urging him back to his solitary life. A return to the quietness of the rugged hills and canyons, where the only sounds were those that came from nature.

"I guess I'd better be on my way," he said, careful to keep his tone neutral.

"No need to hurry off," Dub said gruffly.

"I have some things that need doing, Uncle Dub." The typical excuse of a person who worked closely with animals or the land. Something always needed to be done.

Quint could sense that his uncle wanted to say more, but instead held his tongue.

Dub finally settled for, "Glad you could stay as long as you did, son. Next time, maybe you can stay longer." A wry smile pulled at his leathery cheeks. "By then you'll've had your visit from this magazine lady, and there'll be lots to tell."

"Yeah," Morgan agreed, grinning. "We'll be lookin' forward to hearin' all about it."

Quint said his goodbyes to the women in the house—including flicking little Beth's button nose and leaving a parting word for the absent Erin, Christine's teenage daughter who Morgan had adopted as his own shortly after their wedding— before he headed for the battered ranch pickup parked out front.

He set the twin pound cakes his aunt had wrapped lovingly with aluminum foil on the seat next to him, then glanced over his shoulder through the dust-encrusted rear window into the partially loaded truck bed.

He'd already collected his supplies for the next few weeks, but if he was going to have company for an unknown period, should he make another run to headquarters for some extra things?

His answer was a negative grunt as he turned back around to start the engine.

He might have little say about accepting the magazine woman's company, but no one—not even Mae—had told him to go out of his way to make the experience enjoyable.

In fact, since *she* was the person insisting on gate-crashing his hard-won peace, it would serve his better interest if she didn't enjoy any of it! Then she wouldn't hang around long.

CHAPTER TWO

KATLIN BROWN'S fierce determination suffered a setback as she steered the ungainly motor home into the long U-shaped drive of the Parker family compound. It was one thing to form a plan and something else entirely to carry it out. Especially when that plan involved deceiving people as powerful as the Parkers. From everything she'd learned about them over the past month, they wouldn't take the offense lightly. Yet her purpose was far too important to let temporary misgivings get in the way. Everything she'd been working toward for the past three years hinged on the outcome of these next few minutes. *Everything.*

She took a deep breath, adjusted her grip on the steering wheel, then moments later pulled to a stop in front of the largest house. None of the houses—not this one, or the other four smaller ones sitting opposite each other across a tree-filled courtyard—were in any way ostentatious. A fact that might have come as a surprise, considering the size and reputation of the Parker Ranch. But the scene matched almost exactly the archive photograph she'd found printed along with a couple of equally rare news articles. The Parkers, it seemed, were as protective of their privacy as they were of their land.

Within seconds of her stepping outside, the front door opened.

"Are you Katlin Carter?" a pretty dark-haired teenager asked.

"I am." Katlin flashed a confident smile as she confirmed the false identity. She'd decided to pattern her alter ego after one of the magazine's more popular feature writers—Terilyn Murphy. Terilyn could charm people into sharing secrets that they wouldn't ordinarily tell anyone. Which was what Katlin needed to have happen here. Not with the Parkers, but with *him*. "What's your name?" she asked the girl.

"Gwen. Come inside. Aunt Mae's waiting."

The entryway had a definite Spanish flair. Intricate black wrought-iron lighting fixtures and stair railing continued the front porch theme. Pristine white walls were a stark contrast to several brightly colored rugs scattered on a gray stone floor.

She was shown down a long hall to a private office, where she was asked to wait.

To help keep her nerves ordered, Katlin perched on a couch offset from the door and surveyed the room. The contents spoke proudly of long service and meticulous care. The many books lining the walls looked both well-read and lovingly handled. The rosewood desk, positioned directly across from the door, fairly glowed from numerous polishings.

Silver-framed photographs, undoubtedly of family members, shared space on a nicely appointed table with an art-deco vase overspilling with fresh flowers.

Mae Parker's lair. Mae Parker—the oldest living member of the Parker clan. The matriarch of the family, who, over the past fifty or more years, had garnered a reputation for toughness and determination in the cattle business, in oil and gas leasing rights and in political maneuvering to further those causes. State legislators were known to quake at the mere mention of her name. From what Katlin had learned recently, though, some people seemed to think that advancing age was at last slowing the woman down. That she—

The door swung open and, despite the firm control Katlin held on her emotions, she jumped. She watched, fascinated, as an elderly woman made her way into the room and crossed to the desk. Her posture was erect, her snowy white hair pulled into a smooth knot on top of her head, her navy blue skirt and pale yellow blouse freshly pressed. Her use of a cane was so adroit as to be barely noticeable.

At ninety, Mae Parker continued to impress. Her skin might now share the same qualities as parchment and her body might be less than it once had been, but the iron will and determination that had made her a legend in her own time were in no way diminished. Her personality radiated with remarkable force into every corner of the room.

The woman settled into place at the desk. Only when she was satisfied with the arrangement of her cane did she look up.

"You're late!" she snapped, her words cracking the air like a whip.

"Yes, and I apologize." Instinct warned Katlin to offer no excuse as she rose to present herself.

The old woman's eyes flicked over her. "Did you get lost?" she demanded.

"I took a wrong turn," Katlin replied, then added, "It would have helped if you'd provided better directions."

Without doubt Mae Parker was unaccustomed to censure in her own home, especially from a stranger whose sole purpose was to curry favor. But Katlin knew she had to be direct, almost arrogant. Just as Terilyn Murphy would be in the same situation. Anything less would get her nowhere.

"I've never read a thing you've done, Miss Carter. Not in *Eyes On Texas* or any other magazine."

"This is my first series for *Eyes On Texas.*"

"First *ever?*" Mae demanded.

"I've done other things."

"Who for?"

"Mostly out-of-state publications."

Mae Parker referred to Katlin's letter of introduction, the letter Katlin herself had composed and then signed, using the magazine Chief Editor's auto-signature pen.

"What makes you think you can do justice to this

idea of yours?'' the woman asked, looking up. ''This *Vanishing Texas Cowboy?*''

''I'm interested in the subject. Who wouldn't be? Cowboys have always held a special place in the American consciousness. They—''

''Cowboys aren't vanishing,'' Mae interrupted her. ''At least, not the ones around here.''

''I'll include that in the series, then. If you read Mr. Thompson's letter carefully—my Chief Editor—you saw how I want to offer a true reflection of a modern-day cowboy's life. I want to show not only his day-to-day activities, but why he does what he does. In particular, in the first installment, I want to follow a loner. Someone who spends all his time tending cattle on the farthest reaches of one of the few remaining traditionally run ranches in Texas. I want to observe this man…learn the kind of person he is, see what makes him tick. In the second and third installments, I plan to follow the family men and the others who—''

Mae interrupted her yet again. ''The kind of solitary person you're talkin' about isn't goin' to take kindly to having company.''

''I won't *be* company,'' Katlin countered. ''I'm providing my own shelter, my own supplies. Most of the time he won't even know I'm there!''

''Oh, he'll know, all right,'' Mae countered shrewdly. ''He may be a loner, but that doesn't make him different from any other male when it comes to a female. Have you thought about that?

About what it's goin' to be like when you're out in the 'farthest reaches,' as you put it, and there's no one to run to for help if things were to get out of hand?"

Katlin stood her ground. "I'm sure if I have your permission, no cowboy in his right mind would try anything. Not on the Parker Ranch."

"You think you're that good a judge of human nature?"

"I do," Katlin returned. She didn't add: of *your* nature.

Mae considered her another moment, then asked, "I suppose that thing you drove up in has a lock on the door?"

"A good one, yes. I made sure of it."

Katlin tried not to squirm. So much rested on this seemingly innocuous decision. She had to find a path to her quarry. If this didn't work, she didn't know what she was going to do! It was the best plan she'd come up with that allowed her not only to meet him and talk to him, but to have a natural curiosity about his life. It wasn't just a matter of talking to him, though. She had to have enough time to get *him* to talk to *her* about a subject she already knew he'd want to avoid. A quick sneak onto the ranch wasn't good enough.

"I'm going to have to think about it some more," Mae said at last. "You'll stay for lunch?"

Tension snapped inside Katlin like a broken rubber band, then reformed again—this time even tighter. She drew a taut breath. "Ah, yes. Yes, I will. Thank you." She had no other choice.

Mae collected her cane and stood up. "If you'd like a tour of ranch headquarters Gwen can show you around. No pictures allowed, of course."

"Of course," Katlin agreed quickly.

Mae impaled her with a look. "I assume you will want to take photographs while you're out following your lonesome cowboy?"

Katlin realized she'd made a mistake. She'd been too quick to concede to the older woman. She slowed down. "I'll take a few photos, yes," she answered offhandedly, "but if you'd rather I didn't—"

Mae's frown deepened. "You're awfully accommodating for a magazine person. The last reporter I let visit the ranch took as many pictures as he could get before I put a stop to it."

Katlin lifted her chin. "The material is my priority, Miss Parker, not photographs."

"Awfully accommodatin'," Mae repeated.

"I take pride in being different," Katlin replied, reclaiming her previous arrogance.

Mae accompanied her to the front entryway, where she once again was directed to wait.

The teenage girl soon reappeared. "Aunt Mae said to show you around. What would you like to see first?"

"Your aunt said something about 'headquarters'? I thought *this* was headquarters." Even though

Katlin had spent days searching out information
about the place—and finding, at least, some of the
most essential facts—she thought it best to pretend
ignorance.

The girl smiled. She had wide-spaced gray eyes,
nearly flawless skin and even white teeth. "Well, it
is, sort of. This is where we live, but the actual ranch
office is over there." She motioned to the right.
"So's the bunkhouse, the cookhouse, the barn...the
pens and corrals."

Katlin dug in her purse for a notepad and pencil.
"I knew this place was big," she murmured.

Gwen chuckled as she held the door open. "It's
so big the ranch is split into nine divisions. That's
the only way one person knows the spot another
person's talking about."

A big yellow dog trotted up to greet them.

"That's Junior," Gwen said, stepping off the
porch. "He's Rafe's dog. Rafe's my cousin and the
manager of the ranch. C'mon, Junior," she invited.
"You can come with us if you want. That is—"
She glanced at Katlin, who was straightening from
petting the friendly Labrador. "You don't mind, do
you? You like dogs?"

"I love animals," Katlin said, relieved to be able
to tell the truth.

The dog trotted alongside them as they walked
down the hard-packed gravel drive to a path leading
away from the houses.

"Just how big *is* the ranch?" Katlin asked. "Or is that something I shouldn't ask?"

Gwen countered with a question of her own. "Do you know how big a section is?"

"Six hundred and forty acres."

"Well, the Parker Ranch numbers into the hundreds of sections. Every direction you look from here—for miles and miles—is Parker land."

"How many cattle?"

"You'll have to ask Rafe. Or Morgan. Morgan Hughes is our foreman."

"I doubt I'll see them," Katlin said, hoping fate would spare her that much, at least.

"Rafe's around somewhere. So's Morgan." She glanced speculatively at Katlin. "I overheard Aunt Mae telling Morgan about you last week. She told him she might send you out to Big Spur. That's our most remote division. It's in the hills, much rougher country. Quint McCabe takes care of things there. Quint and Morgan are first cousins. Their mothers are sisters." She laughed. "It gets a little complicated. Like…my last name is 'Dunn,' not 'Parker,' because my grandmother was a Parker and she married…"

The girl continued to talk, but Katlin lost track of what she said after hearing her mention Quint McCabe. The man she'd come so far to find!

She broke into what the girl was saying. "Your aunt said she might send me to Big Spur?"

"She's really my great-great aunt. Yes, that's

what she said. Rafe warned her she's just askin' for trouble, but Aunt Mae told him that was why she was thinkin' of hookin' you up with Quint. Because Quint won't take advantage.''

They stopped across from a group of weathered buildings spread out at right angles around a small clearing. Each rough wooden structure was built low to the ground, with numerous windows shaded by a narrow front porch.

Mindful of her responsibility as a guide, Gwen pointed out what each building was used for, but Katlin wasn't ready to forsake the previous subject.

She broke in again. ''When you heard your great-great aunt talking to Morgan…what did he say?''

''He said he'd talk to Quint.'' The girl veered to a subject of her own. ''My mom's a writer. She's done a couple of children's books—one for older kids, the other for younger. I think it would be a lot more fun to do what you do, though. Go places, meet people, see lots of different things. Mom just plops herself down at the kitchen table.''

''Do you want to write?'' Katlin asked.

The girl shrugged. ''Maybe. I don't know.'' Then she plunged into her tour again, showing Katlin all she thought a visitor might like to see of the working heart of the Parker Ranch. They took a short jaunt through the rather rustic business office, the bunk-house, the cookhouse, the tack room…followed by a continuation of their journey down the path to the corrals and pens beyond. There, for the first time, they saw cowboys. Several men, dressed the part, stood a distance away, clustered outside a corral.

As soon as Katlin saw them she wanted to leave, but her pretense trapped her. As *Katlin Carter* she claimed to be so intensely interested in cowboys that she'd traveled a great distance to be near them. As herself, *Katlin Brown,* the who-what-when-where-and-why of a cowboy's existence was the last possible thing she cared about! She was here for only one purpose…and she wanted to get on with it as quickly as she could.

To her relief, Gwen waved to the men but didn't join them.

The girl explained, "Aunt Mae's starting to get funny about me hanging around the ranch hands. It's weird. I've known most of 'em all my life, but suddenly this summer she's telling me I need to stay out of the way." Gwen grinned. "She's probably tryin' to stop me from doing what Jodie did—Jodie's another of my cousins. She lives in town now, in Del Norte, with her husband, Tate Connelly, the sheriff. They have a new little baby girl, Megan…she's the cutest thing! Aunt Mae doesn't have to worry, though. I'm not goin' to run off with any of these guys. It'd be like running off with Wes—Wes is my brother. And who'd wanna do something like that?"

Katlin eyed her younger companion. The girl was probably about fourteen or fifteen, at the stage where emerging adulthood altered moods and perspectives in milliseconds. Mae Parker could be forgiven for wanting to protect her.

"Your aunt's been around a lot longer than we have," Katlin commented. "Maybe she knows best."

Gwen's eyes widened. "Oh, she'll love that! Someone who agrees with her."

"I didn't say—"

The girl giggled. "Most people think she's a tyrant." She checked her watch. "We'd better be gettin' back. Lunch'll be ready soon." She looked around for the dog, called him away from the corral post he was sniffing, then they turned back. "Jodie tells me the same thing," the girl confided. "Says I shouldn't be in any hurry to grow up. My mom, too. But it's hard when you think you are grown—at least in most ways—and other people tell you you're not. Anna thinks I'm grown up. Anna's my little sister. She's eight."

"Well, you are, to her."

"How old are you?" Gwen asked.

"Twenty-six."

As the girl chatted on, Katlin experienced an almost forgotten spurt of warmth at doing something so simple as conversing, without it being part of a plan. Life wasn't so simple, though, and the reminder she carried along with her was always there. The scar that couldn't be ignored. Gwen had talked about having a brother. Well, she'd had a brother once herself—

"I wish my mom could meet you," Gwen said. "You'd like her. And she'd like you."

"Umm," Katlin murmured, mentally drawing back.

The girl glanced at her, quick to sense a shift.

"Mom's in town with some of the others," Gwen continued. "Shannon and Aunt Darlene, Uncle Gib, Christine—Christine is Morgan's wife—and Delores, that's his mother. They're all at Jodie and Tate's place. They've been fixing up Tate's old house, and Jodie wanted everyone who could, to come by today to see the progress. The house isn't finished yet, but it almost is. They're plannin' a *big* party when it's done."

"You didn't want to go today?" Katlin asked, after an extended silence shamed her into speech.

"Sure I did, but I stayed here with Aunt Mae...to meet you."

The girl shared the information without intent to inflict guilt.

They arrived at the big house and, with Gwen leading the way, went inside.

"The dining room's through there," she said, motioning through a wide doorway. "But if you'd like to wash up first, there's a bathroom down the hall. Straight across from Aunt Mae's office. You know where that is."

"Yes. Yes, I do."

Katlin took advantage of the moment alone in the bathroom to compose herself. For the first time since her arrival at the Parker Ranch she could draw an uninhibited breath.

She leaned against the lavatory and closed her eyes, pressing her forehead against the cool mirrored glass above. She'd known that her audience with Mae Parker would be difficult, but she hadn't expected it to be this extended.

Her lids lifted and she stared at herself, close up. She looked much the same as she always had—her light brown hair short and styled closely to her head, her wide blue eyes, patrician features and slender frame fostering the assumption that she was the product of a sheltered environment—home, parents, schools. Which she had been, until the unexpected knock on the door a little over three years ago changed the world as she'd known it, leaving nothing the same.

She straightened, ran a comb through her hair, then let herself into the hall. Once again, prepared to do battle.

Mae Parker presided at the head of a large table hewn from the same dark wood as its companion sideboard. Gwen, on her aunt's immediate left, looked up and smiled when Katlin entered the room. Mae turned to look at her as well, but didn't smile.

Instead, the woman's dark eyes ran over her, as if searching for something she couldn't quite understand. Katlin wondered how busy the telephone lines had been over the past half hour, between Mae Parker's office at the ranch and the magazine's offices in Arlington. She'd expected just such a check-up call and had made arrangements for cover with Tessa Goodall, one of Malcolm Thompson's assistants. It also didn't hurt that Katlin's last act of careful timing, before quitting her position as a researcher, was to ensure that Malcolm Thompson had already left on his scheduled month-long vacation in Tahiti.

"Did you enjoy your tour?" Mae asked as Katlin took the chair opposite Gwen.

"Yes, I did. Gwen is an excellent guide."

"She tells me you saw some ranch hands."

"Yes."

A middle-aged woman pushed through the swing door from the kitchen and subjected Katlin to an intense appraisal as she distributed individual servings of pasta salad. "Is iced tea satisfactory?" the woman asked.

"Miss Carter?" Mae deferred politely to her guest.

"Yes," Katlin said and the woman disappeared, only to come back moments later with their beverages.

Once they were alone again, Mae returned to her previous subject. "Gwen said you didn't try to talk to them."

"She also said that you preferred her not to be around them."

"*Her,* not you. Why didn't you go introduce

yourself? Cowboys are the reason you're here, aren't—"

"My mother taught me never to be impolite," Katlin inserted before Mae could finish. "It would have been rude to leave her."

A slight, ironic smile touched Mae's lips in appreciation of Katlin's self-proclaimed reluctance to be rude or impolite. Particularly since interrupting an elder didn't seem to bother her. "You're telling me your policy is to dance with the one that 'brung' you…is that correct?" Mae asked.

"That's correct," Katlin said.

"I'm still thinkin' you're a mighty strange magazine person."

Katlin allowed herself a slight smile as well. "I'm sure the concept of using honey to attract a fly isn't new to you."

Mae laughed outright at her impudence. "My dear, *nothing* is new to me."

Gwen had been watching their sparring with great interest. She piped up during the pause, "Katlin agrees with you, Aunt Mae. About me and the hands. She says maybe you know best."

"More *honey,* Miss Carter?" Mae challenged.

"Katlin…please. No, if I didn't agree with you, I'd say so."

Mae held her gaze for a very long moment, before saying, "Somehow, I believe that." Then she glanced at their untouched salads. "Marie will have our hides if we don't appreciate this. Let's eat up!"

Gwen dug in, while Mae ate more slowly.

Katlin also complied, but she couldn't have said either then or later if the pasta salad was enjoyable. She consumed almost all of it, though, in order not to draw attention to herself.

After a light dessert of fresh fruit and cake, Katlin hoped that her ordeal would be over. But Mae seemed content not to hurry.

Sitting back, she directed, "Tell us about your family, Miss Carter. I'm always interested in a person's heritage. Are you from Texas? I'm not placing your accent."

Katlin hadn't expected such a personal question. She searched for something to say...then remembered that the best falsehood always stayed close to the truth. "No, I grew up in a small town in California, not far from San Francisco."

"Is that where your parents live now?"

"Yes."

"I'm assuming you're not married, since you don't wear a ring?"

"I'm not married," Katlin confirmed.

"Brothers and sisters?"

"A...brother."

Despite her best effort, Katlin's throat closed on the last word.

Mae Parker pounced. "Only one?" she quizzed.

"Yes."

"What's his name?"

Katlin stiffened. "I don't see where that makes

the slightest difference, Miss Parker. Frankly, it's none of your business."

Mae was unfazed. "I like to have particulars on the people I let spend time here. Names, addresses."

"If something were to happen to me, call the magazine."

"I already have."

"And?"

"The person I talked to verified that you are who you say you are."

"*And?*" Katlin pressed for a decision. Her nerves were starting to wear thin. She was afraid she'd make more mistakes.

"She couldn't tell me where you'd worked before, either. I find that a little…strange."

"Do you want me to give you the phone numbers of the publications?" Katlin demanded. "I'm not sure they even exist any more, but if you insist—"

"Miss Carter!" Mae said shortly.

"*Katlin,*" Gwen corrected.

Katlin's stomach knotted on the meal she hadn't wanted and on the lies—the many lies—she'd told along the way to get here. But in order to learn the truth about Michael's death, she would do anything! She'd stand toe-to-toe with the devil himself if it meant she could put her parents' minds at rest.

An aggravating mistiness formed in her eyes. She wouldn't look at Gwen, much less at Mae Parker.

"You didn't hear what I said," the older woman offered in a surprisingly quiet voice. "I've given you my permission. I'm not totally happy about whatever it is you're holding back—and I'm sure you *are* holdin' something back—but I'm willing to give you a chance. With one stipulation. I get to see everything you plan to publish *before* you publish it. And that includes photographs.''

Relief flooded through Katlin as she realized she'd won the first battle. She would see Quint McCabe!

Mae's voice intruded on her spurt of happiness. ''But I'm thinkin' I might send you over to Red Canyon instead of Big Spur. Red Canyon will be easier to get to in your motor home. The road's better.''

''No!'' Katlin cried, before she could stop herself. ''I don't mind bad roads. And this Big Spur division...Gwen described it to me and it—it sounds perfect! I want the most remote division on the ranch, the most—''

Katlin's words dried up as she registered Mae Parker's satisfied expression. The suggestion to change divisions had been a ploy, a trap...and she'd fallen straight into it. Mae Parker now knew her interest centered in one place—Big Spur. For whatever reason.

''As you wish,'' Mae murmured, almost to herself.

Katlin could make no reply.

CHAPTER THREE

DUST THE SAME DRY BEIGE as most of the surrounding land billowed to obscure Katlin's vision as she did her best to stay in the pickup's wake. Her arms and shoulders ached from the effort to keep the motor home under control as it bounced over bumps and through hollows on the crudely graded road. Yet she wasn't about to sound the horn to alert Morgan Hughes to a problem.

She had met both of the men she'd hoped to avoid when they'd clomped into the dining room shortly after Mae had given her permission to stay.

Of similar height and lean build, they looked as if they'd come straight in off the range. The only discernible difference between them, when seen through a thick coat of dust, was that Rafe Parker had dark hair and dark eyes—eyes that smoldered his displeasure—and Morgan Hughes had fair hair with pale eyes that looked as if they smiled easily.

"I've made my decision and that's all there is to it," Mae Parker had stated firmly, as if to preempt protest. "Morgan, you're available to take our guest to Big Spur, aren't you? Quint knows to expect her?"

"He knows," Morgan said.

"Good. Then you can start right away. That'll give Miss Carter time to get settled before nightfall, and you to get back home."

"You said you wouldn't decide until after we talked again," Rafe objected.

"What's done is done, boy. Leave it alone."

A silent battle of wills followed, but the old woman's position as head of the family won in the end, leaving her nephew to nod shortly, mutter something to Morgan and stalk out of the house. But not before he'd thrown Katlin a hard look that warned her not to betray his aunt's trust.

Since Katlin had first traced Quint McCabe to the Parker Ranch, she'd proceeded with singular purpose. She was nearing the culmination of her long struggle. She didn't care who she had to go through or around in order to achieve her end.

In her previous life people had been quick to like her. She'd been pleasant and nonthreatening, unwilling even to hurt a fly. She'd never lied or felt the need to calculate. Now she did both well.

She pushed away from the table, saying coolly, "Thank you for lunch, Miss Parker. And for allowing me to do my research."

"Just don't you forget what I said," Mae returned, "because if you do—on purpose or otherwise—you'll regret it."

Katlin's gaze skipped over Morgan Hughes's lean

frame to the girl. "You, too, Gwen. Thank you for showing me around."

Gwen shrugged. "It wasn't that much."

The entire time she retraced her steps to the front door Katlin braced herself to hear Mae Parker say she'd changed her mind, or for Rafe Parker to intercept her and put into words his unspoken warning.

The only person to follow her, though, was Morgan Hughes. He caught up with her just as she was about to climb into the motor home.

"I'll meet you over at the corrals," he said. "In the big parkin' lot out front. Should be a spare pickup around I can use. You are ready to head out to Big Spur, like Mae said, aren't you?"

"I'm ready," she confirmed.

He cocked his head, his blue eyes curious. "Why'd you pick the Parker Ranch? There are other big spreads. Why us?"

"Why not you?" she returned.

Clearly, her glib answer didn't satisfy him, but since the matter had already been settled, he shrugged away his misgivings and said, "I'll see you at the corrals." Then he set off down the path.

Shortly after she turned into the parking lot, he pulled up alongside her in a pale green pickup with the Parker Ranch insignia on its doors. Obviously, he'd had no difficulty commandeering a truck. He warned her to expect some kicked-up dust, gave her the "Honk if you need anything" admonition and accelerated away.

Which was why, even though her arms ached to the point where she'd ordinarily have requested a rest, she wasn't about to give in. She didn't want to hand either him—or Rafe Parker—the satisfaction.

They traveled into increasingly rough terrain—moving out of the relatively flat, mostly grassy valley into foothills where the scattered brush became more dense and the once-distant rugged peaks, mesas and canyons were all around them.

Finally, after what seemed hours, the pickup slowed, then stopped. They'd literally come to the end of the road. A red cliff rose above a wide clearing in an area as wild as any she'd seen. An old trailer with a rusted awning sat to one side of the clearing, while weathered corrals, a couple of sheds, two stunted trees and a small trash heap of discarded items comprised the rest. If this was Big Spur, it wasn't what she'd expected. But then, she hadn't known what to expect.

Katlin parked the motor home at the rear of the trailer, careful to leave a good space between them.

Morgan Hughes stepped out of his truck, cupped his hands to his mouth and yelled, "*Quint!*"

When there was no immediate response he glanced at Katlin, who'd come around to the front of the motor home to watch.

"Is no one home?" she asked drolly.

"I'm here," a man replied from startlingly close by.

He stood in the doorway of the nearest shed. Long and lean, he too was dressed for ranch work in worn jeans, a long-sleeved shirt, scuffed boots and a battered black Stetson pulled low on his forehead. A full western saddle hung at his side, his fingers gripping the horn, while a bridle dangled from the other hand.

When he stepped out of the dimness into full sunlight, his boots scrunching the rocky ground, nothing about the moment felt real to Katlin. Not even as he walked toward her, giving her the first clear opportunity to register what he looked like—undisciplined blond locks poking out from beneath his hat, attractive angular features, a finely chiseled mouth, long straight nose and eyes that were such a pale, pale blue as to be shocking in his sun-bronzed face. Until that moment he'd been as elusive as a ghost...someone she'd heard about but never seen.

His gaze held hers unflinchingly as he drew abreast, and only as he passed by did the spell of unreality shatter. Katlin watched, shaken, as he set the saddle and bridle on the ground and reached to shake hands with the foreman. They, too, were about the same height, with the same lean build. But where she'd guessed Morgan Hughes and Rafe Parker to be in their mid-forties, Quint McCabe could easily be ten years younger.

"How you doin', Quint?" the foreman greeted

him with a friendly smile. "Told you we'd be along."

"Yeah," Quint said. His voice was low, noncommittal.

Both men turned to look at her. Katlin took this as her cue to introduce herself.

"Katlin Carter, Mr. McCabe," she said in a friendly way, continuing the lie. She extended her hand. "Call me Katlin. Don't worry for a second about my visit. I won't interrupt a thing. All I want is to watch and ask a few questions. Nothing difficult."

Two sets of pale blue eyes narrowed against her.

They looked enough alike to be brothers, having similar noses and similar chins. Something she'd been told earlier echoed in her mind. Something Gwen had said.

"Are you two related?" she asked. A good "reporter" question.

"We're cousins," Quint McCabe said, and took her hand in a brief salute that he quickly broke off.

Nothing more was said.

The silence extended.

Morgan Hughes looked from one to the other. Then, smiling slightly, he adjusted his hat and drawled, "Well, I guess I should be gettin' back."

Despite the fact that Katlin had resisted meeting him a few short hours earlier, she experienced a moment's panic when he announced that he was leaving. She might have been a package he'd set out to

deliver. Find the right address, get someone—anyone—to sign for her…then back to the truck, deliv-
ery complete!

"You sure you don't want something cold to
drink?" Quint McCabe offered before she could
think of anything to say.

"Nah. Still got some water in the truck. Miss Carter's lookin' a little grim, though. She might take
you up on it."

Katlin had a good idea what she looked like.
She'd been through a lot that day—the flight from
Dallas to the Midland/Odessa airport, then going
through all the paperwork to rent the motor home.
Not to mention driving it here. "I'm fine," she said.
"I told you, I don't want to be a bother."

"It's no bother," Quint McCabe said and started
for his trailer.

Morgan Hughes called a parting word to his
cousin, but before turning to leave, he took a moment to address her. "Quint's a good man," he said.
"Nothin'll happen out here you don't want to have
happen. Keep that in mind and you'll be okay. If
the loneliness starts to get to you, you're always
welcome to visit Little Springs. Quint'll tell you
how to get there. That's my place, mine and my
family's. It's another division on the ranch, not far
from headquarters."

He smiled, touched the crinkled brim of his hat
and got in the truck.

Katlin had never felt as alone in her life as she

did watching him drive away. He was abandoning her in this place! This, what could only be described as "godforsaken" place in the middle of nowhere, in the company of a man with whom she'd exchanged a scant few words.

"Here." Quint McCabe prodded her arm. When she made a tiny startled noise, he immediately apologized, "Sorry."

"Thanks," she murmured. She sipped the water delicately at first, then followed with larger swallows.

"You can get dehydrated quick out here," he said, "when you're not used to it."

She took a final swallow and sighed. "That was good. I didn't realize."

"Shouldn't ever go far without a canteen handy. Got one?" he asked.

"I brought bottles of water."

"That'll do, I guess."

He lifted his hat to run a hand over his unruly tufts of fair hair, then set it back in place. He seemed curiously unperturbed about her intrusion into his life. Or was it that he could do very little about it, considering Mae Parker had sent her there, and his cousin, the ranch foreman, had deposited her on his doorstep?

She decided to perform a little test.

"I realize my being here is quite an imposition," she said. "So I want you to know, up front, just how much I appreciate your willingness to help. As

I said, I don't want to get in your way. You go ahead and do whatever it is you usually do, and I'll—''

"Do you ride?" The demand cut into her words.

"A little."

"How little?"

She lifted her chin. "I can stay in a saddle."

"Ever ride all day?"

"No, but—"

"Then you're going to get in the way."

"I won't!" she denied automatically.

"How are you going to keep up?"

"That's my worry, isn't it?"

His lips tightened. "No, Miss Carter, it isn't. If you end up a set of bleached bones in one of these canyons, what am I supposed to say to the Parkers? Nope, whether either of us likes it or not, I *have* to watch out for you. You've been put in my care."

"I absolve you of all responsibility."

"It doesn't work that way."

"It does if I say it does!"

"Not on the Parker Ranch. The Parkers set the rules, and I carry them out."

"But—"

"That's the way it is in Big Spur country," he said unequivocally.

"I'll keep up!" she insisted.

He swept his gaze over her and, she could tell, found her lacking.

"We'll see," he said. Then, in a slightly altered tone, he informed her, "I'm not planning anything away from camp for the rest of the day, so if you want to take time to set up your vehicle, go ahead. I'll find an extension cord if you need it for your electricity and a hose so you can hook up to fresh water at that faucet over there.'' He motioned to a pipe sticking out of the ground a foot or two above a dented metal trough filled with water. ''We'll be startin' out bright and early in the morning...six o'clock. Do you usually eat breakfast?''

''I'm perfectly capable of feeding myself.''

''I didn't say you weren't. Just...you should eat something. And bring along some lunch, too. We could be out a while.''

''Fine,'' she agreed shortly.

In an unconscious repetition of his cousin's earlier leave-taking Quint McCabe brushed the brim of his battered hat before going to collect the saddle and bridle. He carried them to the corral, where he draped the bridle over a post, swung the saddle over the top rail, then started to inspect various bits of its rigging.

He'd certainly left her in no doubt that, in his eyes, she was a nuisance, and that it was his intention not to defer to her. Her purpose would be well served, though, if she had to prove herself to him. Because as she showed him that she could stick like a burr and not cause any problems, she could also win his trust.

Katlin closed herself in the motor home and stood at the tiny sink to wash the empty water glass. She wanted to return it in the same pristine condition as he had given it to her.

Then, once again, she experienced a sense of unreality. She could barely believe that she was here. With *him*. And that soon she would learn the truth about Michael.

Michael.

Her thoughts turned to her family as it had once been—almost a prototype greeting-card family. No deep dark secrets hidden away. A few problems, of course, since they were human. But their parents had loved each other and them, and had done their best to give them a good base to carry into their adult lives.

To carry into their adult lives—

It had all started with that fateful knock on the door, the day after she'd arrived home from business school for the Christmas holidays. She'd been in the kitchen, helping her mother prepare for a party, when the front knocker sounded.

"I'll get it," she said, laughter still enriching her voice from a hilarious story her mother had just told.

Flour streaked her face and was on her T-shirt and hands, but she didn't think twice about answering the summons. Her parents had numerous close friends in the area, as did she and Michael. Someone was always dropping by, especially at this time of year. Several of Michael's friends had already checked to see when he'd be arriving. Her brother had missed last year's holidays, unable to leave his duty station. But this year, he would be home. Michael, her own special hero. The one she'd loved dearly her entire life.

She was still smiling as she opened the door and found two men in full-dress uniform on the stoop. Both men were high-ranking officers; the shorter one was a chaplain. Her smile froze at their tight expressions.

"Are you Katlin Brown?" the chaplain asked.

Katlin's heart pounded so strongly she couldn't answer. *Michael!* It had to be Michael! But maybe he was only hurt. Her eyes begged them to tell her that…and their gazes slid away.

"Who is it, dear?" her mother asked, as she stepped into the hall. "Who—?" Her words stopped the instant she saw the two officers. Blood drained from her face.

Katlin hurried to reach her. "Mom!" she cried.

The men, too, hastened inside to help guide her mother to a chair.

"What…happened?" her mother breathed, terror flattening her features. Knowing and yet not wanting to know.

The taller officer cleared his throat and stoically carried out his duty. "Mrs. Brown, we're sorry to have to inform you…"

Katlin picked out the words *killed, line of duty* and *Wednesday, December fifteenth,* but everything else was incomprehensible.

Wednesday…three days ago! She'd been out with

friends that night, celebrating the coming holidays...and all the while, Michael—

A moan escaped her lips.

Her thoughts rushed to her father. "I—my father—he's in the garage. He—he'd want—"

The chaplain murmured, "I'll go," but Katlin said, "No."

She couldn't imagine how difficult it would be for her father to look up from putting the finishing touches on his yard Santa to see the grim-faced officer.

She kissed her mother's damp cheek and walked on numbed legs through the kitchen and into the attached garage. On the way, she removed the baking cookies and switched off the oven. All done in reflex.

From that moment, everything was reflex. As if it was happening to someone else.

She'd never forget her father's face, though, as he looked up, read her pain-filled expression, heard his wife's muffled sobs and put the two together. Or the way, after a second of stunned silence, he stood and, moving through his own suffering, offered comfort to her, to his wife and to the two men who'd been forced to deliver such terrible news at such a happy time. The quiet dignity he'd displayed would stay with Katlin forever.

Friends of the family had surrounded them with love and assisted them through the wait for the body, the military funeral Michael deserved and the empty days that followed.

An accident. In a faraway place. That was all they were told.

Michael had been so proud to be a helicopter crew chief. To care, to the best of his ability, for the machine and the men who flew in it.

The family didn't get the full story, but they did know Michael wasn't the only casualty. Two other families had been given the bad news at Christmastime.

Weeks went by. Katlin hadn't wanted to go back to school. She'd skip the upcoming term, she'd told her parents. It didn't matter. Nothing mattered. However, her father had insisted that she go back to complete her course of study. And, after witnessing his brave composure during the ordeal, how could she refuse him? She earned her MBA and even stepped into a full-time job with the company where she'd interned. The job was too far away from where her parents lived to commute each day. She could only spend weekends with them. As a result, the toll Michael's death exacted from them was more evident to her than if she'd seen them every day.

Both aged faster. Her mother was too quiet; her father never puttered in the garage any more. It pained them that they knew so little about what had happened to their only son.

Katlin took the initiative to learn more. The service owed them a complete explanation. Michael was *dead!*

The answer proved more difficult to obtain than she'd thought. When she pressed for information, then pressed harder when none was forthcoming, another officer—different from the men who'd notified them of Michael's accident—paid a call on a weekday morning when Katlin had been at work. And he'd left them with the not-so-subtle intimation that they might not want to explore the issue further, because if they did, they could learn something they didn't really want to know. He all but told them Michael had been at fault for his own death, as well as the deaths of the other two soldiers.

Her parents were devastated.

As was she. But Katlin was also indignant at the officer's callous disregard for her parents' feelings. When she called to complain, no one she talked to seemed to know anything or wanted to be helpful in any way. She could feel the ranks closing against her and against further inquiry.

Michael had almost seemed like a god to her. Their births had been separated by twelve years, and she'd worshipped her big brother from her first moments of awareness. When she entered elementary school he was a graduating senior, but he'd always made time for her—listening to her chatter and having an interest in everything she did. He'd made her feel special. When he joined the Army she'd missed him terribly and looked forward to his visits home.

He'd been so handsome in his uniform, calling for her at school, impressing her teachers and her friends. He sent postcards and photographs from every place he visited. She was fiercely proud of him. Even as an adult.

Katlin hadn't been able to leave the mystery surrounding his death alone. She *had* to find out if the accident was his fault. He'd always been an exemplary soldier, receiving numerous commendations for outstanding service. From everything she knew of him, he would have never performed his duties negligently, endangering his crew or any of the personnel they were transporting.

She reread his letters, particularly the ones from the past year. She'd jotted down the name of every soldier he mentioned. Then, one by one, she went to see them.

Some were harder to find than others. A few were still in the military; a number weren't. Some genuinely knew nothing about the accident; others had suspicions, but pointed fingers in so many directions their stories were difficult to credit. The hardest to locate were the members of Michael's last crew, both airborne and on the ground. She finally located one person, then another, who, with much reluctance, had independently supplied the same name— Captain Quinton McCabe—as the officer in command of the group on board the helicopter during the "exercise" being performed when Michael was killed. Barely a month following the accident, the man had abruptly left the military. Like her father, Katlin put the two together. She *had* to find this Captain McCabe!

Her job suffered during her personal pursuits, and as a result, she'd left it to do temporary office work, so she could travel easily between assignments.

Her parents hadn't approved, but she'd been driven. She could see how the joy had been leached from their lives, how they'd gone downhill emotionally and physically. The officer's not-so-subtle warning had worked. They didn't want to rock any boats. Yet the possibilities were tearing them apart.

Katlin wasn't out to make trouble for anyone. She was after no one's head or job. She just wanted the truth about Michael's level of responsibility. The real truth. Either way. If he had been at fault, she would live with it. People *did* make mistakes. But if, as she strongly believed, he hadn't been responsible, she wanted to set her parents' minds at rest.

The longer her quest took, the more determined she became. She could feel the changes taking place inside her as she had to use her wiles to find people and get them to talk. She wasn't sure if the friends who'd known her before would recognize her now. If she'd even recognize herself.

She'd caught her father looking at her in a puzzled way on her last visit home. He didn't understand what she was doing, why she wasn't using her intellect and her MBA properly. But he hadn't said anything…because he rarely said anything these days that delved beneath the surface.

It had taken most of two years before she'd gained Quint McCabe's name. Then she'd just about given up getting any further when an anonymous letter arrived, addressed to her—personal and private. It had said McCabe was working on a ranch in Texas. But nothing else. Not what part of the state, not which ranch.

She'd moved to the Lone Star State and found work as a magazine researcher—a perfect ploy to carry on a covert search. Within six months, she'd tracked him down. When Quint McCabe had disappeared after leaving the service, he'd done a good job of it. He'd buried himself so deeply that no stranger looking at him would ever suspect his past.

But she knew. Just as she knew she had to be patient, and, for the time being, maintain her assumed identity.

Her fingers curled around the freshly washed glass.

His glass…the one he'd filled for her.

Before her brother died, had he offered Michael water as well?

A single tear rolled down Katlin's cheek.

Michael's memory was so vivid he might have been there with her, bumping her shoulder with his as he used to when trying to get her to laugh.

To honor his memory, she forced a smile.

Then the smile slipped away. This was a time for mental toughness. She had to concentrate. And at *all* times, she had to remember.

CHAPTER FOUR

THE ALARM BROKE INTO Katlin's deep sleep and she groaned as she reached to turn it off.

The past night had been horrible. Coyotes yipped and yowled from what sounded like right outside in the clearing, their eerie racket making the hairs on the back of her neck stand on end. She could imagine a pack of the wild beasts sniffing around, seeking her out…and all that stood between her and them was the motor home's thin layer of aluminum siding. Other noises also had made her cower. Flaps and screeches, snorts and smacks, rustlings in the brush that ended occasionally in a tiny cry of startled surprise.

She'd been exhausted before falling into bed and had needed desperately to find rest, but she hadn't slept until sometime after two o'clock. Now it was five—barely three hours later. It wasn't enough! She'd set the alarm unnecessarily early. He'd said six. She could afford to lie still with her eyes closed, just a little longer, and still be ready for—

Something crashed against the side of the motor home. The noise wrenched Katlin awake. Jerking upright, she blinked into the grayness.

"It's six o'clock," a man's voice called. "Are you ready?"

Quint McCabe!

Katlin's head swung around. The clock confirmed his words. What had—? How had—? She remembered waking up earlier...then drifting off again.

A series of sharp whacks caused the door to vibrate. "Are you *alive* in there?" he demanded.

"Ah— Yes! Yes, I'm alive!" she called as she leaped out of bed to tear into the jeans and shirt she'd set out last night. "I'm—I'm just finishing. I won't be a minute."

She dropped to the floor to pull on her socks and western boots. She'd bought the boots only a few weeks earlier; they weren't broken in enough to push her feet inside easily. After a hectic struggle, she rushed into the bathroom, raced through a quick toilet, then combing her hair, detoured through the kitchen to grab the rucksack she'd loaded last night with water and half a peanut butter sandwich. Then she tumbled outside.

"I'm ready!" she claimed, though she felt nothing of the kind.

He looked at her steadily, his handsome features set. He wore much the same clothing as he had the evening before, only with the addition of long leather chaps, a worn denim jacket and a faded bandanna that he'd tied loosely around his neck. His hat, of course, was pulled low on his forehead.

"Is that a new style or something?" he asked, motioning toward her midriff.

Katlin looked down to see that her shirt buttons were off-kilter. "No," she said and quickly corrected the oversight, starting at the bottom button and working her way up.

He motioned to the rucksack hung over her shoulder. "Your food and water?"

"Yes, I—"

He took it away from her before starting for the corral. As she hurried to keep up, he opened the flap to investigate. "This all the water you're bringing?" he asked.

"A couple of bottles...surely that's enough."

"We can get a refill at a tank if we have to, I suppose." At her puzzled expression he explained, "We use wind power, Miss Carter. Windmills to suck the water from the ground and tanks to hold it for the stock. Water's a precious commodity out here. What's this?" He held up her plastic sandwich bag.

"Lunch," she said. "You told me to bring something to eat."

"You didn't have time for breakfast. I know, because I heard you scrabbling around in there. This isn't enough."

"I don't eat very much as a rule."

"You will out here."

"I know what I'm capable of eating. I—"

Katlin's protest broke off as they reached the corral, where two saddled horses waited, their reins looped around the top pole. One was brown, the other gray. He went straight to the brown horse and pulled a set of saddlebags from across its back. He handed them to her, along with the rucksack.

"Be easier if you switch your things into this. And while you're at it, find something else to eat, too. And bring along a jacket. Just in case."

"Anything else?" she asked with clipped astringency.

"Nope, that'll do," he said, and turned to complete his own preparations at the side of the gray horse.

Katlin gritted her teeth as she walked back to the motor home. It irritated her to have *him* tell her what to do. She might have been a new recruit being dressed down for inexperience. It irritated her even more, though, to have gotten off to such a bad start.

She made a second half sandwich of peanut butter and jelly and threw in an apple for good measure, even though she doubted that she'd touch either. Then she found a cotton jean jacket similar to his and pulled it on since the morning air still held a chill. Her own contribution to the saddlebag collection was a baseball cap, which she had a good idea she'd need later as protection from the sun.

He glanced up briefly on her return. "That's better," he said, and went back to what he'd been doing. This time he made no move to relieve her of her burden. He seemed to expect her to deal with it.

Katlin eyed the brown horse. She wasn't as accomplished at working with horses as she'd claimed. She approached the animal carefully. Then, attempting to emulate Quint McCabe's previous action—only in reverse—she lifted the bags to set them back in place behind the saddle. But instead of remaining still, the horse skittered sideways, keeping her at a distance.

"He's called Chili," Quint McCabe said, having stopped to watch her. "He's a first-rate cutting horse. You ever ride one?"

Katlin looked at him blankly.

"A cutting horse," he explained, a muscle tightening in his jaw. "One trained to work cattle."

"No—I—are they different?"

Her answer didn't please him. "Just…get on," he said flatly. "The sun'll be up all the way soon. We need to get moving."

Sealing her lips, Katlin stepped up to the horse again, swung the bags into place, planted her foot firmly in the stirrup and bounced into the saddle—all the while hoping she came off as looking competent.

Her entire lifetime riding experience consisted of the three lessons she'd started on the same day she'd bought her boots. Her mount had been of the rent-a-horse variety, one who had walked the same trail so many times he could do it in his sleep…and possibly had, considering the number of times she'd had to thump his sides to encourage him to keep moving.

This horse—Chili—danced around with lively steps, forcing her to grab the saddle horn to keep from falling off.

Quint McCabe shook his head as he took control of the horse, quieting him with a soft word and touch. Then without warning, he grasped her lower leg and held it against the animal's ribs. "Stirrup length looks about right," he said, "but let's check. Stand up."

"What?"

"Stand up, so I can see."

Katlin stood, feeling odd.

"All right," he said, satisfied, and signaled for her to relax. Then he secured the saddlebags in a way she hadn't known to do, untied the horse's reins and handed them to her. "You might need these," he commented dryly.

His tone told Katlin she'd committed yet another faux pas. Her hired mount had always been waiting for her, just as this horse had been, the stirrups always seemingly the correct length since no one had ever checked. The reins, too, had been given to her by her "instructor," a teenage girl who, from that point, had done her best to sulk through the next half hour.

Quint McCabe mounted the gray in one smooth motion, and the horse, anxious to be off, moved away almost as soon as his rider's foot was in the stirrup. Quint quickly pulled the horse around and directed him to wait.

At a glance Katlin saw that he carried far more gear on his saddle than she did on hers—coiled ropes, some kind of thick-skinned carry bag and a rifle tucked into a long scabbard within easy reach.

She didn't have time to dwell on the significance of the weapon, because Chili, responding to the activity of the gray horse, moved off as well. He didn't go far, though. After a few steps he began to toss his head, sidling and turning, his metal shoes striking rock and stirring up swirls of dust.

Katlin's heart leaped to her throat. She didn't know how to deal with the powerful animal. How to make him stop! She hung on as best she could, tightening her grip on the reins, until the horse, backing up, gave an abbreviated rear.

Quint McCabe's sharp words were for *her*. "No! Don't pull back on the reins! Keep him moving forward. Don't pull back!"

He brought the gray close and seized the reins, forcing her to release her fearful grip. Once again, he spoke softly to the horse, "Whoa, boy. Whoa, whoa, whoa."

"Just how much have you ridden?" he demanded, once the situation was again calm.

"I'm not used to this kind of horse!" she protested, embarrassment making her defensive.

"Lady, this is the only kind of horse we have out here! The Parker Ranch isn't an amusement park. Horses have to know what they're doing, just like people do. If he's too much for you to handle, say so. You don't have to come along. Just so long as you don't wander off. People have been known to get themselves lost in these canyons and never find their way out. And that's the God's truth.''

"I'm going with you!" she insisted.

"How, when you can't ride? There aren't any roads in the places I'm heading. You either ride or go on foot. I'm not walking and you won't be able to keep up on the ground. I'm advising you to stay.''

"Would you hand me the reins, please,'' she requested tightly.

His pale eyes, more visible now that the grayness of premorning had given over to the pinkening hue of a rising sun, were narrowed. She couldn't tell what he was thinking and didn't really want to know. But she wasn't going to be left behind!

"Tell me what to do,'' she said, in effect admitting her amateur status.

He was silent a moment, then said, "Ease up. Don't hold the reins so tight. The horse doesn't like it and he doesn't need it. He wants to work. It's what he's trained to do.''

"All right,'' she agreed. "Anything else?''

"Let's just move on. See what happens.''

"He won't throw me, will he?'' Katlin couldn't rid herself of the memory of the frightening moment earlier.

"Not unless you do something awful to him.''

He handed her the reins again. And while she waited for him and the gray to move a few steps away, she took what she hoped was an undetectable breath, then tried to make peace with the horse.

"Chili," she murmured, "let's do this, okay? It's really important."

She tapped his ribs and the horse moved forward—only to play up once again, skittering and twisting and shaking his head.

"Remember what I told you," Quint McCabe said firmly. "Loosen up on the reins. Get him to do what *you* want. Turn him to the left. Pull left and keep pulling left."

Katlin did as he said, and the horse immediately settled down. Soon they made an awkward circle, then another smoother one.

"Okay. Now try going straight," Quint instructed her.

Katlin made the correction and this time the horse moved forward, catching up to, then falling into place beside the muscular gray as he and his rider started down the graded road at a slow walk.

Gradually, Katlin began to feel more secure. It was nice not to have to keep reminding her mount to move forward. Nice to be sitting so high and to hear and feel the rhythmic clomp of hooves on the ground. She was so absorbed in the moment that she didn't notice Quint McCabe had turned off the road until he gave a low whistle.

She looked back.

"We're going this way," he called.

He and the gray horse were partway down a long

brush-filled slope. With seemingly no clear path, the brush looked high enough in places to reach her boots. A variety of tall spindly cactus also sprang up here and there, sending numerous arms twisting Medusa-like from the ground toward the sky.

Katlin's dawning confidence faltered. She was doing all right on level ground....

She pulled Chili around and the horse turned obediently.

As she drew near where the gray horse had left the road her disquiet must have shown.

Quint McCabe said, "Your horse is surefooted and will pick the easiest way up or down. Another thing...most all the stuff you see growing out here either sticks, stinks or stings. Remember that if you decide to get down."

"Doesn't it hurt the horses?" she asked.

"This isn't easy country for anybody, horses included. They're used to it, though. They were born and raised on the ranch."

"Still—"

"Do you want to go back?" he cut in irritably.

"No," she said.

"Then stop talking."

Katlin's jaw snapped shut as she pressed the horse to follow him.

Without exchanging another word, they worked their way down that slope—surprisingly managing to thread their way through. Then up and down numerous other slopes, into canyons and gullies, and through draws where rock outcroppings shaded them from the steadily rising sun.

More than once Katlin had to stop herself from crying out. When a descent that had initially looked simple proved to be anything but. Or when a thorn snagged her jeans and ripped skin as well as cloth.

She never saw a cow or anything else alive in the beginning. She, Quint McCabe and the horses seemed to be the only living beings in this huge silent land.

Then, gradually, she started to notice little things—grasshoppers leaping away from the horses' hooves, lizards sunning themselves on rocks, and, on occasion, small birds flitting from bush to ground and back again. She also came to realize that their seemingly aimless wandering had purpose. The occasional flashes of reddish-brown that were little different in color from some of the rock outcroppings, turned out to be white-faced Hereford cows, almost always with calves. As soon as the mother cow spotted them, she'd be off, her baby close behind. They'd disappear into the shadows or into a clump of thick high brush, or around the side of a large boulder.

Katlin was accustomed to seeing cattle in photographs or grazing in pastures alongside the highway, seemingly content to spend their days ambling slowly and peacefully along. She'd never seen a cow take flight before, amazingly agile on the stony ground.

She almost commented along those lines to Quint McCabe, but was glad she hadn't when she recognized that this was what he'd been doing all along— noting each and every elusive cow and calf.

As the sun rose higher, so did the temperature. Katlin peeled off her jacket and draped it across the front of the saddle. Then, shifting position, she licked lips that were growing steadily drier. Her arms were still sore from battling the road yesterday, and now those aches had been joined by others, particularly those in a more southerly location.

Quint McCabe twisted around to check on her— for the first time that she was aware of.

"Ready for a break?" he called.

She nodded assent.

He pulled up in a small clearing beside a tumble of rocks and was out of the saddle in one smooth motion. Still holding the gray's reins, he caught hold of Chili's bridle to steady him while she followed suit.

Katlin dismounted, but with nowhere near the same ease. Her spine didn't want to straighten, her rump felt bruised.

"Time for some water, don't you think?" he said. "I was waiting for you to say something."

"You told me not to talk...so I didn't."

"You can get things out of your saddlebag while you're riding, you know. One thing for sure, you're not going to run into the back of anything when you're on a horse. It's not like driving a car."

"I think I'll have my sandwich now," she stated stiffly.

"Sure thing. Go ahead."

Katlin retrieved one of her half sandwiches and a bottle of water.

"What about you?" she asked, uncomfortable with the knowledge that she might be the only one eating.

"I had breakfast," he said.

"What time is it?" In her haste she'd forgotten her watch.

"About nine-thirty."

"Is that all?" she asked, surprised.

He took the horses off a few paces to tie them to a sturdy branch in a small thicket of mesquite. Then retrieving his canteen, he came back to her.

Katlin leaned against a large rock and watched as he took a long drink. "It seems later than that," she remarked and tipped water into her mouth as well— water that tasted more wonderful than anything she remembered drinking in a long time.

"Time has a way of moving slow out here."

She bit into her sandwich and before long it was gone.

"What are you doing today?" she asked. "Why are we out here?" She thought she'd worked that out already, but she needed to ask questions.

A sudden gust of wind rustled through the mesquite.

"We're checking pasture," he answered. "Seeing

what cattle we can stir up, seeing what condition they're in. Pretty soon we'll be repairing a length of fence that I know needs some work. Then we'll probably make our way over to the nearest windmill, check out it and the tank, and on the way there we'll check more cattle and more fence. Sound entertaining?''

''What are you looking for when you check the cattle?''

''Injuries, illness…to see if any have obvious problems.''

''What do you do if you find a sick one?''

''Try to help it.''

''How do you do that?''

''Give it medicine, apply a salve or a powder…do whatever's necessary.''

''How do you catch them? The ones we saw earlier—''

''You sure ask a lot of questions.''

''Isn't that my job?''

''You tell me.''

''I asked how you catch them,'' she repeated.

''Rope 'em.''

''What about the mother? She stands around and waits while you—''

''She's well armed and knows how to use 'em.''

''You mean—''

''You have to watch that she doesn't try to hook you with her horns. Depends on how protective a mother she is. Some go a little crazy if you mess with their babies.''

"Then how do you?"

"I liked it better when you were quiet."

Katlin finished her water and pushed away from the rock. "All right," she said. "Let's get on with it."

His eyes moved over her. "You sure you don't want to go back to camp?"

"No."

He went to collect the horses.

Katlin folded her jacket to stow in the saddlebag, but before putting it away, she retrieved her baseball cap. She was just slipping the cap on after adjusting the sizing so it wouldn't blow off in another errant gust of wind, when Quint McCabe came to stand at her side.

"You need a leg up?" he asked.

"A what?" she said.

"A leg up…to get back on the horse."

She shook her head. "No, I'm fine. I can do it."

He shrugged and moved to remount himself.

Katlin paid for her refusal a moment later when she dragged herself back into the saddle. She settled into as comfortable a position as she could manage and steeled herself to carry on. No word of complaint would pass her lips, no matter how bad the situation. Yet even in her discomfort, she sensed that this departure would be easier. She had learned much about dealing with a horse, both in the way she gave directions and in letting herself trust his ability to make good decisions.

Feeling she owed Chili something to make up for their bad beginning, she patted his neck and said gruffly, "Good boy."

If Quint McCabe heard her, he made no comment.

Katlin shifted position periodically as they moved on, trying to lessen the hurt in one area, until that area started to hurt as well.

For a time they followed the path of a dry, cracked creek bed, bleached almost white by the sun. But, eventually, they came upon a wide valley where even her untrained eye spotted a distant line of barbed wire fence.

Quint McCabe headed straight for it.

All along, she'd had a perfect view of his back— following him, watching him. His posture was ramrod straight, yet at the same time relaxed. No matter how hard she tried, she couldn't copy it.

Something caught his eye, though, because he stopped the horse to peer off into the distance.

Katlin drew up alongside him. "What is it?" she asked.

"Buzzards," he said shortly.

She searched the sky in roughly the same quadrant and spotted a number of dark specks gliding gracefully in a loose circle. "Are they doing what I think they're doing?" she asked.

"They've found some lunch. We'll go check."

Almost before the last word was out of his mouth,

he urged the gray into a canter. Katlin hesitated for only a second before signaling Chili to follow. It was all she could do to hang on when Chili quickened his pace as well. She gritted her teeth against the pain.

Lunch turned out to be a dead Hereford cow. Several of the large birds had already dropped out of the sky, their naked red necks and heads bobbing as, one after another, they pecked the soft flesh.

Quint pulled up a short distance away, barked, "Stay here," to her, then urged the gray forward again.

The birds flexed their great wings as he drew nearer, warning him off. When their show of prior claim did no good, they managed another greedy peck or two, before lifting back into the air.

Quint stepped down from the gray to examine the carcass.

Katlin watched as he studied it, her stomach turning slightly. She was relieved to be where she was.

A moment later he straightened, remounted, gave a sweeping look around, then rode back to her.

"She had a lot of rings on her horns, which means she's got some age on her," he said. "A small udder, too, so she probably didn't have a calf this year. Musta managed to miss getting picked up during culling. Couldn't escape the end of her wily days, though. Can't hide from that."

"You're not going to leave her like this, are

you?'' Katlin asked. ''The buzzards—'' She looked up at the circling birds, then quickly away again.

''Buzzards have to eat, too. They're just as much a part of nature as we are.''

''But—''

''You want to dig the hole?'' he challenged, but didn't wait for her answer. He urged the gray back into an easy canter and retraced the way they'd come.

''What were you checking for just now?'' Katlin asked once she caught up to him. Her voice bounced in concert with her bottom as it slapped the saddle.

As if realizing that the faster pace was difficult for her, he pulled the gray back to a walk. ''I wanted to see if I could tell what happened to her.''

''Why?''

''To make sure it's not something that could spread in the herd.''

Katlin frowned. ''You said she died of old age.''

''That's my guess.''

''What else could it have been?''

His pale eyes turned on her, like lakes of water in a thirsty land. She could tell he didn't like talking…to her, or probably to anyone. A man didn't live alone in such an isolated place if he appreciated conversation.

''One thing's screwworm,'' he said levelly. ''Ranchers thought they had it beat, but a case turned up in the state last fall. Morgan's spread word to keep an eye out. Never seen a case myself.

Haven't had it here on the Parker Ranch since some-time in the mid-seventies, but from what I've heard, it got pretty bad back then in the whole Southwest. A number of ranchers lost a lot of cattle, and there wasn't much any of 'em could do, except doctor it as fast as they found it.''

"What, exactly, is screwworm?" she asked. His previous reply had been the most he'd said since she'd arrived. She wanted to encourage him.

He threw her another estimating look. "You sure you want to know?"

She nodded. She could tell by his expression that this was going to be rough. He didn't expect her to like it, but he would give her every detail, just to see if she could take it.

"Screwworm's a special kind of flesh-eating maggot. A screwworm fly will lay a bunch of eggs into a scratch or cut...and she lays so many that, unless it's treated, the larvae can kill a cow or calf within a couple of weeks. Eats 'em up alive. Digs in, likes fresh flesh. A lot of larvae means a lot of new flies...and the cycle takes hold until cold weather sets in and kills the flies off.''

Katlin swallowed. "You said...back there...it wasn't that.''

"Nope.''

"How can you tell?''

"No flesh missing except for the few choice bits the buzzards got. No bad odor, either. Morgan says there's usually a distinctive smell.''

Katlin wanted to stop talking about it, but curiosity drove her on. "So...if it was so bad back then, how did they—the ranchers—get rid of it?"

He smiled. "A miracle of modern science. They flooded the whole region with sterile screwworm flies. Animal Health people discovered that it messes up their reproduction...and, eventually, no more adult screwworm flies lay eggs."

"But you said there was a case last fall."

"Found and treated, and probably followed by a release of more sterile flies. There's been no new reports that Morgan's heard. Still, we check to be on the safe side. So do all the other ranches."

"What were you thinking to find when you looked around? Another dead cow?"

"Mostly I was making sure she didn't have a calf. If it was born this spring it wouldn't be big enough to survive on its own. It'd still depend on her for milk and protection."

A whole new world was opening for Katlin. A world she'd never given any thought to before.

"What would you do if you had found a calf?" she asked.

"Depending on its condition...bring it back to camp and feed it. Maybe take it to headquarters where they might have some other orphans they're taking care of."

Katlin turned to survey the scene behind them, then she settled back around. "But that cow didn't have a calf, you said." She wanted reassurance.

"It's doubtful," he said.

"But...if she did—"

"Then the coyotes or the wildcats will have a nice meal tonight, or they've already had one."

"That's...quite callous."

"It's nature. One animal's misfortune means another animal will survive longer. The cattle out here have pretty much reverted to wild. They've learned to fend for themselves. On smaller ranches where the owners have smaller herds and each and every calf makes a difference to their financial year, they pamper them from before they're even born. Out here...the Parkers have so many cattle spread over such rough country—their Hereford line goes back to around the turn of the last century—we can't possibly find each and every one, even with twice-a-year roundups. We try, but look at the place. You can see why some get missed."

His little speech seemed to tire him out. Either that or he'd again become impatient with her questioning. Because, seconds later, he cut ahead of her, and once again presented her with his back.

Katlin nursed her growing aches and pains and tried not to think about what he'd said.

She didn't want to get interested in the way a ranch operated. She didn't care about the life of a modern-day cowboy.

She was here for only *one* reason.

CHAPTER FIVE

THEY MADE THEIR WAY BACK to the barbed-wire fence, then turned to follow it to the place Quint McCabe wanted to repair.

Katlin found it increasingly difficult to sit still. When he finally pulled up, she vacated the saddle as quickly as she could, ignoring everything but her pressing need.

"I take it the bathroom is in the bushes?" she asked.

"It's the only one I know about," he said.

"Then...that's where I'll be," she murmured.

"Don't forget what I said about things sticking and stinging. And keep an eye out for rattlers. They grow pretty big out here."

"I'll take my chances," she retorted and hurried off.

In some areas, the valley floor was thick with brush. In others, the principal vegetation was grass. Luckily, this section offered a mix and a good screen of bushes wasn't far away.

Quint McCabe whistled as he prepared for work. Katlin didn't know whether he was doing it to re-assure her that he was still there, or as a homing device, in case she got turned around. She wished she could be completely free of him, just for these few moments, but the prospect of getting lost out here, particularly on foot, had absolutely no appeal.

Katlin minded her every step as she slipped behind a cluster of tall bushes. She wasn't sure how she would react if, at the most vulnerable moment, a coyote paid a call, or a cow showed up, or even a rabbit surprised her. The break proved uneventful, though, and after readjusting her clothing, she headed back to where he still whistled. The tune broke off shortly after she reappeared.

"What's happened here?" she asked, digging into the saddlebag for her second bottle of water. Up and down the arrow-straight line of fence, the four strands of barbed wire were taut. In this spot, the wires sagged between two listing wooden posts.

Quint McCabe righted one of the posts and jiggled it, as if testing to see if it was still in one piece. "Cows always seem to think the grass is greener on the other side."

Katlin compared the two pastures. "They look the same to me," she said.

"*You* aren't a cow."

He worked from both sides of the fence, scraping dirt back into the hole with his boot and tamping it down. Then he went to the second post and repeated the process. Only when both posts had been stabilized did he start to deal with the loose wire—hammering new staples onto the top line of the next post down the row, then attaching an odd-looking metal implement to both post and wire.

"You need to stand back," he directed. "This stuff can sure bite if it gets away."

"What are you going to do?" she asked as she retreated.

"Stretch wire."

A moment later the top line was taut, and with quick assured movements, he secured it with staples to the now erect posts. Then he repeated the process on each successive line, until this section of fence was indistinguishable from the rest.

"It…looks good," she murmured, unsure how he would react to a compliment.

He gathered his tools without comment and stowed them in his saddlebag. But instead of remounting, as she'd expected, he turned and asked, "Are you hungry again?"

"I could eat," she admitted, finding, to her surprise, that she could.

He took a thick meaty sandwich from the second bag and, without ceremony, started to eat.

She ate standing up as well, though she knew that their reasons were vastly different. He wouldn't have the same difficulty as her sitting down. Nor would he be concerned that he might not be able to get up again. His energy level seemed as high now as it had been when the day started. Whereas hers— She stifled a yawn, her nearly sleepless night taking its toll, as well as the morning spent outdoors.

"You ready?" he asked upon returning from his own short visit to the bushes.

Katlin nodded. She started to take another quick sip of water, but stopped. This was the last of her supply; only half the bottle remained.

"You see why I said you'd need more water?" he demanded.

"Do you hear me complaining?"

"No, but you will."

"You said something about a windmill?" she reminded him.

"You still want to go on?"

"Definitely!"

His gaze moved over her—intent, yet impossible to read.

"All right then," he said and swung effortlessly back into the saddle.

Katlin dragged herself back up on Chili again, muffling her reaction. Her posterior had passed "abused" some time ago. It now moved into full "battery."

Quint signaled the gray to move on.

A short time later they came upon the windmill, its gently whirring blades announcing its presence—loud in a land that, up until then, had seemed filled with silence. Chili moved a little faster of his own accord, as did the gray. Both horses sensed water and were quick to dip their noses into the cement stock tank as soon as they reached it.

Katlin was ready for a drink as well, having finished off the last of her supply, but she hesitated to share with the animals.

Quint McCabe didn't pause before splashing water over his face and head and wetting his bandanna.

He looked at her, water droplets glistening on his hair and bronzed skin as he rubbed the bandanna on the back of his neck. ''Won't hurt you.'' He smiled encouragement.

She stared at the light growth of moss on the bottom and sides of the tank. ''I can't drink this,'' she said tightly.

''Even if you'd die otherwise?'' he challenged.

''I don't know. I might, if—''

''Do you think you can afford to be so picky? We're a long way from camp.''

Katlin continued to gaze at the water, licking her lips. She wanted it and yet—

''Your choice,'' he said shortly, and scooped a handful of clear liquid to his mouth.

Katlin edged closer. She touched her fingertips to the water, then slid her hands in. It was cool and wet and wonderful. She dabbed some on her face, on her neck, and breathed a joyful sigh. But she still couldn't bring herself to drink it.

''There's a pipe over there,'' Quint McCabe said at last, motioning to a section of tank closest to the windmill. ''It's where the water flows in. You'll have to work at it, but it's straight from the ground. If that suits you better.''

"Thank you," she murmured and hurried over. She drank thirstily before refilling her bottles.

"Same water," he commented flatly, as she stored the bottles in her saddlebag.

"Like you said, in some things I'm just...picky."

He grunted, refilled his canteen by dunking it in the tank, then took the horses over to a small weathered enclosure and shut them inside.

"I have to check something," he explained before heading off.

"What?" she called after him.

Either he didn't hear her or he didn't want to answer. She watched as, after stopping the windmill's slowly turning blades, he climbed the tower, stepped off onto the narrow platform near the top, fiddled with the mechanism, then, after a time, started down again.

Katlin held her breath the entire time. He made it seem so simple. But the structure looked about as substantial as a child's stick toy and if he'd fallen from that height—

Her first thought was of her unasked questions, the ones that were so vitally important to her family. Then she thought of him and wondered if she could have helped. He'd been working on the ranch for three years, though. Maintaining windmills was obviously something he did on a regular basis.

Once he set the blades free and started back to her, she asked coolly, "Was there a problem?"

"There was. There's not any more."

"You fixed it?"

"No, I checked it. I fixed it a couple days ago."

"You doubted your work?"

"No," he replied again levelly. "I doubted the mechanism."

"You don't have much of an accent," she slipped in, thinking it time to get personal. "Why not? Everyone else around here does."

"Maybe it's because I didn't grow up around here."

"Where then? Where did you grow up?"

He collected the horses from their short rest, checked their girths along with other straps and bits of bridle, then mounted the gray. All without answering her.

"I have Mae Parker's permission to ask as many questions as I want," Katlin informed him as she struggled into the saddle.

His smile was tight. "Bet she never said I had to answer 'em." Then he tapped the gray's sides and again left her to follow.

THE AFTERNOON FADED into a blur of heat and increasing exhaustion as Katlin kept up only through sheer force of will.

Almost in a daze, she remembered seeing cows and calves. Sometimes they were in pairs, sometimes they banded together in small groups. All continued to flee if they came too close.

Occasionally, Quint had instructed her to stay put

while he took a closer look, and she'd watch as, in concert with his horse, he'd catch up with a group of escaping cattle and work to separate a selected calf from its mother—no easy feat when neither wanted to be separated. The gray, seemingly with little or no direction, bent his head and haunches in opposite directions to block the calf's determined attempts to return. Each time the calf feinted, the horse, snorting fiercely, shifted course, anticipating the calf's every move. At that point Quint would decide whether to let the animal go, having seen all that he needed, or to treat him. If the calf needed treatment, a loop of rope flew out like magic to capture his neck. Frightened, the calf would try to dart away…only the gray had already stopped and braced himself, and when the animal hit the end of the rope, he flipped himself over backward. Quint yelled and waved his hat at the mother cow, to scare her off. Then, bouncing down from the saddle, he'd heave the calf back onto the ground if it had struggled up, bind its legs quickly and administer whatever medication was needed, all the while keeping a wary eye for the mother's return. In seconds the calf was free, loudly bawling his complaints. Quint would then canter back, and after shaking the wrinkles from the rope, recoil it and return it to the saddle. Then he'd resume the lead and they'd be off again.

Katlin told herself she could do this! She could

wait and watch and continue to ride. Ride all day—all night!—if she had to.

But soon she stopped noticing cattle. Either they hid more successfully in the many draws and canyons, or she was beyond caring.

Feeling herself sway, she clutched at the saddle horn.

He, of course, didn't notice. She could have plopped to the ground any number of miles back and he wouldn't have known or cared.

The way he kept going and going—

Quint McCabe was a hard man, hard like the land. Spare with words, trained by both the military and his harsh existence not to expect compassion or give it. Would he even listen when, eventually, she made her appeal?

She thought of the way her parents' lives had frozen into the moments after they learned of Michael's death. How they functioned as prisoners of a possible truth that they were afraid to question.

She swayed again as the day suddenly darkened, and this time, felt herself fall—

QUINT HAD KEPT A CLOSE WATCH on her all day. At least, as close an eye as he could manage without her realizing what he was doing.

Her very presence had irritated the hell out of him from the beginning. He didn't want her to think she was getting any kind of special treatment. He wanted her gone from Big Spur. As the day wore on, though, and she repeatedly refused to return to camp, he'd been forced to relent a little in his opinion. She was miserable…but she wouldn't quit.

A magazine writer. Recent to the state from the sound of her. And she'd had the nerve to question *him* about *his* accent?

He glanced around in time to see her sway. She righted herself but didn't look particularly steady.

He felt a niggle of unease. He was accustomed to the hardships of riding pasture; she wasn't. She'd gotten exactly what she'd asked for, though—to accompany him through his daily work schedule. Yet he'd have done more if she hadn't been along. So, in the end, he *had* made concessions. He'd been forced to, once he discovered that she could barely ride a horse.

He held Jim back and slipped into place beside her…and got there just in time to catch her as she pitched sideways.

"Whoa!" he quickly directed the horses, and sensing that something was wrong, both animals stopped short.

Quint looked at the woman crumpled helplessly in his arms, half in and half out of the saddle. Wildly differing emotions raced through him. Anger at her, because through her own stubbornness she'd created yet another problem, and a disquieting awareness of her soft femininity. Her cheeks were flushed, her hair disheveled—she'd lost her Oakland A's baseball cap sometime back.

He checked to see whether she was suffering from the heat, and was relieved to find that the skin around her mouth was moist, as was her forehead, so her body hadn't lost the ability to cool itself. She was just completely worn out.

Removing his bandanna, he managed to dampen it with water from his canteen and bathe her face and neck.

She started to come around as he finished.

"Don't—what—what are—?"

He was struck by how blue her irises were. Almost a violet. And the thick curling lashes surrounding them were naturally a darker shade of brown than her hair. She had no makeup left after the day she'd spent. He was seeing her without artifice. The soft smooth skin, the delicate shell-pink lips. All natural.

Once complete awareness returned, she jerked free of his arms and righted herself in the saddle. "What happened?" she demanded, her cheeks an even brighter pink as she looked around, blinking.

"You just about fell off your horse," he informed her.

"I didn't! I—"

He smiled tightly. "Lady, you're talking to the person who caught you."

She licked her lips, then licked them again.

"Do you have any water left?"

"Yes." She produced a bottle that was about one

third full, which she emptied in a few long swallows.

"Was that the last?" he asked.

She nodded.

"Then it's a good thing we're almost back at camp."

Her gaze made another search of their surroundings. "We are?"

"About ten minutes away."

"But...nothing looks—"

"You wouldn't recognize it. We came back a different way."

"Ten minutes?" she repeated.

"Think you can make it?"

"Of course. Just now—I didn't—"

"Let's go," he interrupted her. "Before you wear yourself out again."

He urged Jim into a slow walk and brought Chili along with him.

"I can steer!" she fussed, still slightly muzzy as she tried to retake the reins.

He avoided her reach. "You just concentrate on staying put in the saddle."

She sputtered some more, but stopped resisting. Possibly because her energy had flagged, or because she finally understood that what he'd done all along was for the best.

He made no secret of keeping a close eye on her as they covered the short distance back to camp. She still didn't seem particularly steady, and he was relieved when the small settlement came into view. So was she. She looked like someone glimpsing heaven after a particularly bad day in hell.

Even the horses seemed relieved to have the day over. After he set them loose in the large holding pen adjoining the rear of the corral, both were wallowing in the grass and dirt, massaging their backs, before he had time to place their sweat-drenched saddle pads over the fence to dry. He watched them for a moment, smiling, then turned to take the riding gear back to the tack room. Only to find that his companion for the day had made little progress from the spot where she'd dismounted.

"What's up?" he asked, careful to keep his tone neutral. She'd accepted his offer of help down, but rejected further assistance. He'd known she was covering for her embarrassing condition, so he'd left her to it. He understood pride, even if, in this instance, he thought it misplaced.

She explained tightly, "I can't walk. I have a cramp. Could you please—"

"Help?" he supplied. "Sure. Be glad to." He slipped an arm around her waist. "Where's the cramp?" he asked as they started off.

"I'd rather not say," she returned staunchly.

He smiled in spite of the sure knowledge that he shouldn't and murmured, "Oh…there."

"We'll get through this a lot easier if you don't gloat!"

"Don't you mean *you* will?" he charged dryly.

Her body stiffened, instantly prompting a groan.

He reached for the motor home's doorknob, expecting it to turn. It didn't. "It's locked," he said, frowning.

She dug in her jeans for a key. "Of course."

"Why? There's no reason. Who would go inside?"

"Still…"

And from her tone, he knew that tomorrow the door would be just as securely locked. Though he doubted that she'd be up to riding again so soon. At least, she wouldn't if she had any sense.

He stepped into the motor home and turned to help her in—lift her in, actually. The living space was so small the pair of them seemed to fill it. Awareness again swept through him. Only stronger this time.

"Anything else I can do?" he asked, releasing her.

She limped to an eating nook a few steps away, and carefully, painfully, lowered herself onto a cushion. "No thanks," she said curtly. "You've already done enough."

As if this whole cockamamie idea had been his, not hers! *He* wasn't the one who'd insisted on tagging along where he had no business. "If that means you think I did this to you on purpose—"

"Did I say that?"

"You implied it."

She braced her shoulders as if prepared to argue

further, but in the end, she took a breath and said, "I'm in your debt, Mr. McCabe. If I sounded ungrateful, I apologize."

The words were correct, but something about the suddenness of her capitulation, coupled with a certain evasiveness of tone, set off alarm bells.

She met his look with those dark blue eyes that shifted so easily to violet, and he felt his suspicion fade. She had no idea who he was or what had brought him to this place. She might be affiliated with an arm of the media, but her intention was to write a magazine puff piece, not a hard-hitting exposé about a botched military operation.

"Apology accepted," he said gruffly. "And the name's Quint."

After an awkward moment where neither said a word, Quint let himself outside.

He was out of practice with women, he decided as he walked back to the corral. For the past three years he'd limited his contacts with women to the Hugheses and the Parkers, and that during only the shortest of visits to headquarters. Kisses were on cheeks, smiles free and easy. It had been a long time since his senses had tried to overtake his will. Since he'd felt drawn to the way a woman moved, spoke, looked, smelled.

He glanced again at the motor home and wondered if she, too, had noticed him. Then he couldn't help but laugh at himself.

Maybe next time the other ranch hands invited

him to join them in their romantic pursuits across
the border, he should go. It'd be a hell of a lot better
than acting like the love-starved coyote that he was
right now!

KATLIN SLUMPED AGAINST THE TABLE the moment
the door snapped shut. Could she have made a worse
beginning? She'd been on the wrong side of the picture from the very first moment and had done little
to improve the bad impression all the way through
the day. Then, near the end, to almost tumble out of
the saddle into his arms. And finally to have to ask
for his help to the motor home!

What a mess!

She'd wanted to prove herself to him, and had
ended up proving…what?

She groaned as she shifted position. Her body felt
as if she'd gone over a waterfall in a barrel…and
crashed onto rocks below. Every muscle ached. Her
head pounded. Her neck was beyond stiff. She never
wanted to see a horse again. Or a rock, or a cactus.
Even her eyelashes hurt!

How could she go on?

She answered her own question. She couldn't. At
least, not right now. The best she could do about
anything at the moment was to limp into the bathroom, stand under the warm shower spray and hope
it would erase a tiny portion of her pain. Following
that, she'd fall into bed and sleep.

If the same pack of coyotes was to prowl close to the trailer again that night…and if they happened to find a way inside and wanted to eat her…they could. She had nothing left to fight them with.

CHAPTER SIX

KATLIN WAS AWARE of nothing until her alarm rang at five-thirty the next morning. The last thing she wanted was to get back on a horse to repeat what she had yesterday, but she was determined to go through with it, if that would stand her in better stead with Quint McCabe. She knew he wouldn't expect her to show up, which was exactly why she felt it so important to be there, ready to go.

At first, movement was agonizing. She donned a clean pair of jeans and a fresh shirt, crammed her feet back into her boots, packed a more substantial lunch, then forced herself to eat breakfast. She also set out extra water bottles. She would not be caught short again. Then balancing the collection on her folded jacket, she started for the door.

Now if she could only figure out how to bring along the proverbial pillow to perch on…

The morning was still gray as she stepped outside. The air was fresh and cool, with a hint of sweetness. A light was on in his trailer, signaling he was up.

Soft noises came from the corral—a horse snuffling, the chink of spurs. She followed the sounds and found Quint McCabe saddling the horse he'd ridden yesterday.

His face registered surprise at seeing her, but he soon went back to securing the various straps and buckles.

"Good morning," she greeted him, doing her best to sound chipper.

"Morning," he returned, without looking up again. He wore much the same as he had the past two days—jeans, chaps, boots, bandanna, jacket, hat.

"I was wondering," she said. "Do you have an extra hat I can borrow? Mine disappeared. I lost it out there somewhere." She motioned vaguely in the direction they'd ridden yesterday. "It can be old and battered. I don't mind. And, possibly...some chaps?" She laughed, trying to make light of her request. "Chaps aren't something I even *thought* about bringing."

Finally, he stopped what he was doing. "Do you actually think I'm going to let you go through with this?"

She pretended not to have heard. "I never realized what chaps were for. I thought they were just part of the 'look.' There's some pretty vicious thorns out there that I'd just as soon not come into contact with anymore. I—"

"You don't have to worry, because you *aren't* coming," he said firmly.

She took a breath. "I'm up, I'm dressed. I don't see why—"

"Because I say so. And out here, I'm boss."

"But Mae Parker—"

"—isn't here," he finished.

"The whole idea is for me to observe what you do!"

He led the gray out through the corral gate, then mounted the eager horse, that he immediately had to hold back. "You can't *observe* what I'm doing if you're flat on your back for a week, which could easily happen if you beat yourself up again today. It won't bother me any not to have you along, but I bet it'd sure as hell bother you."

Katlin stepped away from the dancing hooves, still clutching her bundle. She knew what he said was true, but she hated having to admit it.

His pale eyes pierced her in the morning gloom. "Whatever I do is sure to need doing another time. You won't miss anything if you get some rest today. Just don't wander off."

Katlin murmured a reply, but he'd already released the horse and cantered off, heading in a different direction from the one they'd taken yesterday.

She started back to the motor home, and had managed only a few limping steps when she noticed the light still on in his trailer. Had her appearance disconcerted him so much that he'd forgotten it?

She knew the door was unlocked. *Who would go*

inside? he'd asked yesterday. *Who, indeed?* was her response today.

The opportunity was too good to let slip away. She knew so very little about him. She could take hours to look around, if she wanted. She just had to be careful not to disturb anything.

Katlin changed destinations. If he came back and caught her, she could use the forgotten light as an excuse. She was only doing him a favor.

The knob twisted easily and the door swung open. A voice inside her castigated her for what she was about to do. It was wrong to invade a stranger's home, wrong to infringe on his privacy. But this wasn't *any* stranger. And her only purpose was to learn more about him.

Was he married? Divorced? Did he have children? She could use any information she could glean as a way to bond with him.

Photographs, letters, cards… Anything.

What she discovered on the surface told her nothing. Except that he kept order in his surroundings and he liked to read. Paperbacks filled every available space. Books that covered a wide range of subjects, from light humor to popular novels to biographies.

As she moved from room to room in the long, narrow enclosure, she saw no photographs or cards of any kind. No letters to him or from him, waiting to be mailed. Nothing that told of a wife or a sweetheart, or even hinted that he'd once had a military career.

She took a deep breath and searched deeper, pulling open drawers and closets, and nosing into cupboards. She found nothing except clothes, household supplies and, finally, a bankbook.

The bankbook gave her a quick tingle, until she saw that it reported an account in nearby Del Norte, with an amount incapable of stirring any excitement.

He might not have had a past.

He might have been exactly what he held himself to be.

She switched off the light and stepped outdoors. Disappointment weighed on her. As did all the effort she'd expended. She was sorer now than when she'd started. She didn't even want to think about how additional long hours in the saddle today would have made her feel.

She hobbled back to the motor home, crumpled into bed, then, with a frustrated sigh, went to sleep.

THE SUN HAMMERING down on the motor home made the sleeping area as hot as an oven. Katlin knew the instant she awakened that she'd forgotten to fully open the windows. With a groan she corrected the error, hoping for a fast exchange of air. Which was when she saw him ride in.

As was fast becoming a habit, she checked the clock. Could she have slept the entire day? Surely not! Then she saw that it was only a little past noon.

He'd come back early? Why?

She took another shower to help with her aches and pains, then went outside. She found him in one of the storage sheds, hefting a saddle onto what looked to be an ancient sawhorse.

"You're back early," she said. She was a little uncomfortable talking to him so soon after having "broken into" his trailer, but she shrugged away guilt because she'd done it with the hope of furthering her cause. She wondered if he'd remembered leaving on the light, and had been confused when he returned to find it switched off.

"I did all I needed," he said, then stepped past her to go outside.

Katlin trailed after him. "Because if you came back early for my sake…as you can see, I'm perfectly all right. I'm sore, but—"

"Don't you mean your butt's sore?" he tossed over his shoulder.

She gazed at his back. A joke? From him? She smiled slightly. "Yes, well…"

"First time's always the hardest," he said.

"Was it hard for you…the first time you rode all day? Or did you grow up on a ranch and ride all your life?"

He covered another step or two, before swinging around to face her. "You forgot something when you were in my trailer."

His words caught her off guard.

"Your lunch, your water, your jacket." He ticked off the articles.

"I—I must have forgotten them when I turned off your kitchen light. You'd left it on, you see, and I didn't think—"

"They were in my bedroom."

Katlin had a vague memory of setting the bundle aside when she began her more extensive search, then she hadn't thought of it again.

"I—I—"

"Did you think I'd left on more lights? Or, since you were already there, did you decide to have yourself a little look-see? Just couldn't resist. Reporter's disease."

She glommed onto the excuse. "I—yes! It was rude of me, I know. But I thought—I know what it's like in the motor home, and I wondered how you managed in such tight quarters. Being here month after month. You have quite a lot of space, though, don't you? I mean, in comparison to what I have." She hurried on. "A separate living room and kitchen, space to walk around. It's really quite…roomy."

He looked at her. She couldn't tell whether he believed her or not. But if he chose not to believe her, what could he do? She hadn't taken anything. She did her best to withstand his scrutiny.

"Next time," he said shortly, "ask."

"Oh, I will. Not that I plan for there to be a next

time. I saw everything I needed. I was just curious, that's all. I didn't mean to offend.''

"People out here don't like being taken advantage of. You never go on a man's land without his permission, just like you don't mess with his hat or put a rope to his cattle. Not even if his cows have wandered onto your land. You pen 'em up and call him. That's the way things are done.''

"I'm sorry.''

A small silence extended.

"Why don't you come get your things?'' he said. "They're not doing any good where they are.''

She followed him the few yards to his trailer and waited under the awning while he disappeared inside.

"Here you go,'' he said, handing her the bundle.

"Thanks,'' she murmured and turned away, angry with herself for having been so careless.

She wanted him to trust her! Not become more suspicious.

She could feel him watching her—consideringly?—as she limped off.

WHEN KATLIN RALLIED her spirits enough to go back outside, she found Quint McCabe sitting in the shade of his trailer awning, patching a pair of scuffed leather chaps. A good portion of one section had been ripped almost apart and he was putting it back together.

Despite how silly she might look, Katlin had

brought along a cushion. His outside chairs were old and metal and offered absolutely no relief for a tender bum. She'd also dusted off her Terilyn Murphy winsomeness and charm.

"Do you mind if I ask some more questions?" she asked brightly.

His hat, bandanna and spurs were nowhere to be seen and she wondered if he felt naked without them.

"Would it do me any good if I did?" he countered.

She made a place for herself in the chair next to his.

"Well, first...I probably should ask a few things about the ranch. I know the place is so huge it has nine divisions. Gwen explained that back at headquarters. But...how big is Big Spur itself? Yesterday, we seemed to go on and on."

"Most people would consider Big Spur a ranch on its own."

"And you're the only person who tends it?"

"It pretty well tends itself. I mostly keep an eye on things."

"But you do this by yourself, right? Don't you get lonely?"

"Sometimes."

"You're not married?"

"No."

She grinned. "A girlfriend?"

"I thought this was going to be about the ranch?"

"My series is about cowboys. Cowboys and ranches go together, don't they?"

"Can't have one without the other."

"You said something yesterday about a roundup. What, exactly, is a roundup?"

"You're a city girl, aren't you?"

"I'm from a small town, but it's close to a city."

"A roundup is when we gather cattle."

"Why? What for?"

He smiled slightly at her pressing curiosity. "In late spring we find all the cows and calves that we can, process the calves—get 'em branded and vaccinated and such—then they're let go again so they can grow. In the fall, we round the cattle up again, and the ones that aren't kept for the herd are sold. That's a simple explanation, but it's what's done."

"And cowboys do all that work?"

"Wouldn't get much done without 'em. Not on a ranch like this. The cowboys flush out the cattle from where they're hiding and move 'em from one place to another, then the ones that are being sold are weighed and put on trucks. Takes about a month each time to do everything."

"And you work the roundup, too?"

"I help. All the regular ranch hands do. Plus some extra men Rafe or Morgan bring in. We go into an area and sweep through it, collecting all we can."

"How many cattle are there on the ranch?"

"Can't rightly say."

"A thousand?"

"Multiply that by ten or twenty, and maybe you'd be close."

She whistled softly. "How many are in Big Spur?"

He shrugged and repeated, "Can't say."

"Can't...or won't?" When he remained silent, she scratched something in her notebook, then asked, "The Parkers sell their baby calves?"

"Those 'babies' usually weigh about four hundred and fifty pounds by the time they're sold. But, yeah, they sell 'em. Some they hold onto for another year to sell as yearlings."

"What about the calves you checked yesterday? They looked small standing by their mothers, but when you stood next to them, they were bigger than I expected."

"Momma makes 'em look small."

He shifted in his chair and she immediately shut the notebook. She didn't want to push things too far.

"That's enough for now, I think," she said. "This gives me a good start on understanding. Thanks."

As he watched her go through the slow process of rising, he demanded, "Why are you doing this when you don't know anything about it? Why not write about something you know?"

She grinned. "I don't have to murder someone to write a murder mystery, do I?"

She arched her back to loosen the stiff muscles...then noticed that his eyes had dropped to her breasts. They stayed there for only a few seconds, but the effect was electrifying.

Katlin immediately straightened, while he busied himself with the leather chaps. The moment might not have happened.

But it had.

IF KATLIN HAD BEEN at the ranch under normal circumstances—if she actually was who she said she was and planned to write the cowboy article—she would have left Big Spur right then. The best way to prevent any kind of unwanted sexual attraction was to nip it in the bud. To not let there even *be* a bud. But she couldn't leave. She *had* to stay. So she would have to deal with the attraction, and the only way to do that was to get control of herself.

He was nice-looking, yes. More than nice looking, with his lean cowboy looks, light hair and pale blue eyes. But in this instance, his looks fit the old song she remembered—something about not knowing the devil had blue eyes and blue jeans....

Mae Parker's warning about there not being anyone to run to if things were to get out of hand suddenly had more force. But things wouldn't *get* out of hand, because she wouldn't let them!

He was lonely. She was lonely. That explained everything.

She was...lonely? Her life was full of purpose. For the most part of three years she'd dedicated herself to finding out the truth about Michael. There hadn't been room for anything else. Or anyone. There still wasn't. Particularly him!

QUINT LEFT THE CHAPS on the chair and went inside the trailer. If he was a drinking man, he might have downed a short one. It had been all he could do moments before not to close the distance between them, and find out for himself if she felt as good as she looked.

Her action had been unconscious, and she'd ended it as soon as she'd seen that he'd noticed, but not before he sensed that she'd found his attention pleasurable.

He couldn't help but laugh at himself again, though. Only this time with less incredulity. There *was* something there. And she'd felt it, too.

He couldn't settle, so he strode back outside. He needed to do something active. Something that would take his mind off thoughts of her.

She was a magazine reporter, for Pete's sake, and he held a secret close to himself that a reporter— any reporter—would love to delve into. He didn't think she had an inkling, even though the first chance she'd gotten she'd gone through his trailer. If the excuse she'd given wasn't the full truth, it was close. She was curious about him because of her article. It wasn't anything to do with Manzant or what had happened there, or anything to do with Colonel Tucker.

He opened a box of horseshoes, found the other

things he needed, then left the tack room to collect Jim.

She'd been partially right in thinking he'd returned early because of her. He had. He didn't think she should be left on her own all day, not as badly as she was hurting. But he'd also returned early because Jim had thrown a shoe and it needed to be replaced.

KATLIN WENT OUTSIDE again almost immediately. She wasn't about to stay hidden away. She'd seen Quint walking across the clearing to the corral with some tools in hand, and knew she couldn't let another opportunity for conversation pass by. Each time she managed to get him to talk, she moved a step closer to her goal. As for the other thing…she was ignoring it.

The gray stood inside the corral, waiting patiently as Quint secured his halter to the top rail.

Katlin came to watch from the other side, not far away.

"I thought you were resting," Quint said. He seemed very careful about where he put his eyes.

"I saw you walk by and I was curious."

"I'm just gonna shoe old Jim here."

"His name's Jim?" she asked, her gaze moving over the gray horse.

Quint nodded. He patted the horse's rump, then began to rub all the way down the animal's hind leg. He seemed to be alerting him to the fact that the leg would be lifted. Then in a practiced move Quint stepped over the leg as he lifted it—facing away from the horse—grasped the foot tightly, positioned it between his thighs and started to clear dirt from inside the hoof. Next, using long slow strokes from a rasp, he smoothed any cracks from the horny rim.

"Kinda like getting your fingernails done," he said.

"Seems kind of dangerous for the manicurist," she commented.

He smiled slightly at her quip. "When you stand like this, you can feel the leg start to tense…and if you do, you let go quick."

"Or the horse will kick?"

"Oh, he'll kick. You just don't want him to kick *you*." He dropped the rasp and reached for a metal shoe that he'd placed nearby. "Jim's been doing this for so long, he can practically do it himself."

She watched as he slipped some flat nails between his teeth, tested the shoe's fit, then drove the nails in at an angle with a small hammer. He worked slowly, carefully, and Jim never turned a hair.

"I don't think I'd like someone doing that to me," she told him.

"Only way to keep the shoes on. Each one is about fifteen ounces of steel."

He checked his work, let the leg go, then released the gray from the halter, letting him run free in the corral. He laughed softly as Jim showed off, performing feints at imaginary calves.

Katlin smiled, too. "I thought you had to have an anvil and a fire, then do all kinds of work to make a shoe fit."

"I try to keep ahead with spares I've already sized."

"Kind of like a shoe store?" She grinned.

"Exactly."

The brown horse nickered softly, anxious to gain their attention. Quint walked across the corral to let him through from the larger area in back. Chili trotted straight toward her.

"Does he remember me?" Katlin asked, laughing as the horse thrust his head over the top rail.

"Sure. You two got to be pretty good friends yesterday, didn't you?" Quint came to stand at the fence, but still on the opposite side. Which was preferable to Katlin.

"I'm not so sure about that," she said, tentatively touching the horse's nose. "Chili probably thought he'd drawn the short straw when he was afflicted with me."

"You started out rocky, but you got better," Quint said.

Katlin glanced at him, then away.

Jim ambled up, wanting to get in on the attention. Quint scratched a spot on his belly and the gray smacked his lips.

"Aren't there any girl horses?" she asked.

"Mares aren't used for work, only for breeding. And the only males we use to work cattle are geldings. Geldings keep their minds on what they're doing. They're the only ones you can trust."

"You never use stallions? In all the old movies—"

"There's a world of difference between what goes on in movies and what happens on a real ranch. A stallion's got one thing on his mind. He thinks his job is to get every mare he sees pregnant and he does his damnedest to make sure it happens."

She skittered away from such a vivid image. "You said Chili and Jim were born on the ranch? Does that mean the Parkers raise horses too?"

"For work, yes."

"*Everything* here revolves around cattle."

"That's what happens on a ranch."

"There are different kinds of ranches. Some are wild animal parks, some cater to tourists."

He shrugged. "Different ways to make a living…but they're not cattle ranches. Not like this one. The Parkers keep to tradition as much as possible, where most modern cattle ranches don't. That's what sets the Parker Ranch apart. It helps to be in this section of the country, too, with plenty of room for cattle to range on their own. A few oil and gas wells don't hurt either."

"I'm sure." She continued to rub Chili's cheek and to stroke his neck. Her body was growing weary of standing in one place, but Quint was talking without as much reservation. She wasn't about to say she wanted to stop. "What do they do that's different?" she asked.

"Mostly, it's what they *don't* do. When we collect cattle, we don't use motorcycles or four-wheelers or…helicopters. We use horses that have been born and trained on the ranch. When we want to move cattle from one area of the ranch to another, we don't truck 'em, we trail 'em. We don't run the spring calves through collapsible chutes to do all that needs doing. We do it the old-fashioned way, with crews of men. I've never cowboyed any other place, but most of the men have and they like this way best. But it's a lot of hard work."

She'd noticed his hesitation on saying *helicopter,* but didn't draw attention to it.

"You've only worked here?" she asked.

He avoided a direct answer. "There are two types of working cowboys—the ones who move around, and the ones who stick in one region or place, if they like it."

"Which means you like it."

He nodded.

She chanced another personal probe. "How long have you been here?"

That was it. That did it. He closed up.

"Long enough," he said crisply, and shooed the horses back to the larger corral.

He didn't return when he finished.

CHAPTER SEVEN

THE NEXT MORNING Katlin was nowhere near as sore. The day of rest had worked. She still had some residual aches and pains, but could function despite them.

She made the same preparations as she had the mornings before, and presented herself at the corral.

Once again, she found Quint readying Jim, but she noticed Chili had also been brought into the smaller enclosure.

Quint's gaze flashed over her. "I didn't think you'd be willing to wait another day."

"No, I'm much better."

"Hat's over there." He motioned to where the second saddle straddled the rail. "So are a pair of chaps. They belonged to the man who used to look after this place. He was a lot lower to the ground than I am, so they should fit you fine."

Katlin went to the rail and lifted the scuffed leather chaps. They were the same ones he'd been working on yesterday—the long rip now fully repaired.

She held them out in front of her, measuring the fit. They reached the top of her boots.

"They'll do," he said.

"How do I?" She didn't know how to get into them.

"The belt buckles in back, then you do up the snaps on the leg."

She wrapped them around her middle, awkwardly threaded the buckle, then bent to connect the snaps. She managed the first few, but had a hard time connecting the one below her knee.

"Here," he said, brushing her hands away.

She hadn't realized that he'd moved! Startled, her first instinct was to step back, but he'd already hunkered down to finish the job.

A wave of awareness washed over her. Impossible to prevent. Impossible to ignore.

She turned away quickly as he straightened, blood rushing into her cheeks. She forced herself to concentrate on the hat. She'd told him looks weren't important; it could be old and battered. The tan Stetson was both, but it fit almost as if it had been made for her. Another legacy of Big Spur's previous overseer? And if pulled low on her forehead, the brim would shield her face, not only from the sun but from him.

She took a few steadying breaths and crossed back to where Quint was saddling Chili. The chaps flapped with each step.

She waited until he finished before smoothing a hand down Chili's neck and loading her supplies in the saddlebags. Once again, she'd been sure to bring plenty of water.

"We need to set some ground rules," Quint said, after he led the horses out of the corral. "When you get tired, say so. Don't wait until you're ready to drop. When you want to turn back, tell me. Even if we've only been out a half hour. There's nothing you can do about being in the way…you are, just by being here. So we'll work around it." He paused, as if expecting a protest. When she remained silent, he said, "At most, this will be another half day. I don't think you should do more."

"Agreed," Katlin said as she pulled herself into the saddle. Muscles and tendons that had been quiet to that point set up another cry as she assumed the same position that had injured them.

He offered her the reins, and her skin tingled where their fingers brushed.

Then he mounted Jim, and instead of urging the horse into a bone-jarring trot, he kept him to a gentle walk. He still struck out into the lead, but turned periodically to check on her.

THE GRAY OF PREMORNING evolved into a salmon-pink dawn. As dawn was replaced by full daylight, they moved into an area Katlin had never seen before. Canyons were wider, cliff walls were lower, boulders displaced large rocks, and the slopes were nowhere near as steep.

From what Katlin could tell, Quint seemed to be

checking cattle again. He had yet to stop to inspect any cows or calves, but she could see him note this one or that one.

"Don't you ever get tired of doing this?" she asked.

"It's what I do," he called back.

"But...don't you ever get tired?"

He reined in Jim until they could ride side-by-side, then he motioned to the wild beauty of the land around them. "How could a person ever get tired of this?"

"Yes, but—"

"Eighty-mile vistas when you're in the right spot, nature at its unspoiled best, a quietness that almost hurts as it fills your soul. It spoils you for anything else. The hardest thing to get used to when you leave is all the noise people make."

"There's plenty of noise here, believe me!" Katlin countered. "My first night—" She stopped, unsure if she should go on.

"What happened?" he urged.

"I thought the coyotes were going to break down the door and eat me!"

He smiled. "Nah. You'd put up too much of a fight."

"They sounded like they were right outside!"

"Probably a mile away, at least. And a pair can carry on until you'd swear there's a couple dozen."

"They don't eat people?"

"Not unless you look like a field mouse or a jack-rabbit. That's their specialty."

"But you said they'd eat calves."

"Weak ones, sure, and anything else that's easy prey. They'll bring down a healthy calf, too, but usually only when they've been driven into strange territory and they're hungry."

"So I don't have anything to worry about."

"Nope." He glanced at her. "What do you know about buzzards?"

Katlin's heart speeded up. But only because he'd voluntarily asked *her* a question, revealing a certain progress in their status.

"Do you mean…do I think they'll eat me?"

"Yes?"

"Well," she said carefully, wanting to win more points, "they're scavengers. They only eat things that are already dead. It's not like the old cliché where buzzards circle someone staggering through the desert, waiting for him to die so they can pounce."

"Takes a full day or two of whatever-it-is lying there, before they get interested."

She tilted her head. "Are there animals out here that I *should* be wary of?"

"Bobcats and mountain lions, javelinas and rattlesnakes—"

"What's a javelina?"

"A wild pig. Likes to move around in the brush.

Got tusks that you don't want to mess with. Near-sighted, though.''

"So I could run away?"

"You could try."

She tilted her head. "Are you trying to frighten me?"

"Then there's the cattle themselves. You've seen a cow's horns. Haven't seen a bull yet, but they're around.''

"You *are* trying to frighten me!"

He shrugged, grinning. "You wanted to know what it's like to live out here."

She moved in the saddle, trying to find a comfortable position. "Do you think we could take a little break soon?" she asked.

"Sure," he said, then something caught his attention and he stiffened, his eyes straining ahead, past a clump of brush.

They rode forward to investigate and Katlin finally saw what Quint had. A cow, standing her ground, not running away. A short distance beyond the cow was the calf she was trying to shield. Small and bony, it lay on its side, barely able to lift its head. The cow became even more intent on protecting her baby as they drew nearer.

"Oh!" Katlin cried. "Poor thing. What's the matter, do you think?" she asked Quint.

,   "It doesn't look good," he said flatly. "Get back a bit. I'm going to have to scare her off."

He grabbed his coiled rope and waved it in the

air at the same time as he urged Jim toward the pair. The cow lunged, doing her best to drive a horn into Jim's stomach. At a touch of Quint's spur, Jim spun away and the cow stabbed empty air, causing her to stumble. As she strove to maintain her balance, man and horse swung around for another charge. Between Jim's snorting and snapping and Quint's yelling and slapping rope, the cow took fright and rushed to escape.

"Yell out if she comes back," Quint ordered Katlin, before bouncing down to examine the calf.

With a shake of his head, he took the two steps back to Jim and pulled the rifle from its scabbard.

Katlin watched for the cow even as she kept one eye on Quint. When he pumped the rifle lever as he circled the calf, looking for a suitable angle, she dragged her gaze away. Two missed breaths later the rifle fired, making Katlin jump.

Within seconds Quint had replaced the rifle, remounted Jim and started back to her.

Katlin drew a shaky breath, audible enough for him to hear.

"Had to be done," he said quietly. "It was either that or let the calf suffer. Mother's real young, probably a first-time heifer—first time she's had a calf. Probably had it late and wasn't able to feed it proper. Little baby never had a chance."

"So…it was going to die for sure?"

He nodded again. "Too far gone to help."

Katlin drew another shaky breath. "I'm not—"

she began, stopped, then completed, "I'm not used to that."

The mother cow came back, sniffed her calf cautiously, bawled once, then scampered away again.

"C'mon," he urged. "Let's ride up here a ways and take that break you wanted."

Katlin nodded agreement.

QUINT FOUND THEM some shade under a scrub oak and helped her down. Then he saw to the horses.

"Here," he said when he returned. "I thought you might want to sit on this. You can have mine, too." He held out the jacket she'd put away earlier and offered his as well. "Make the rocks a little softer."

"Thanks," she said with a flickering smile.

She folded the jackets, placed them on a flat rock, then carefully lowered herself.

"Here's something else," he added, tossing her one of her water bottles.

"Thanks," she repeated, and took a sip.

He opened his canteen to do the same.

Katlin looked around at the hot, dry land, and for the first time appreciated its stillness. She didn't think she could stand any kind of noise at that moment.

A feeling Quint McCabe seemed instinctively to understand, because he stood, not making a sound, looking out at the land as she did, letting the silence encompass them.

Some time later—she had no idea how long—she shook herself and said softly, "I'm not upset that you had to do it…just that it had to be done."

"Only the strong survive out here."

"What about her? Will she have another calf?"

"Next spring. She could already be pregnant. The bulls are out."

"Does everything here revolve around pregnancy?" she demanded, suddenly irritated, though she didn't know why.

"A cow in the pasture with a calf is what it's all about. Without that, you don't have anything."

"And you cowboys would be out of a job."

"Well, yeah, I guess so." He glanced at her. "*The Vanishing Texas Cowboy* would really vanish."

"There's always rodeos."

His laugh was somewhat rueful. "Not much that rodeos and ranch work have in common, either."

He'd caught her attention. "Why not? I thought—"

"It started out that way, ranch hands getting together to show off what they could do. Friendly little competitions. But the whole deal changed over time to what it is today."

"What's different?"

"Working cowboys don't ride bulls, for one thing. Or break all the wild horses the way they show. Don't get down off a horse much, either, unless there's a need. And there's never another cowboy riding along to make sure the calf we want to rope keeps going straight. Things like that."

"You don't like the way rodeos are now?"

"They're mostly for show. I don't mind. Just…they're not real. Some real ones around for the working cowboy, but they don't get the big press the flashy ones do."

"What about the cowboys who compete in the flashy ones? Aren't they real?"

"They might've been at one time. Might even have a spread of their own. But they know the difference. They're in it for the money and the notoriety. Some call it a sport."

"You don't like money and notoriety?"

"Nope. I like it here."

"Where it's quiet."

He smiled and Katlin felt her heart speed up again, this time for a reason she didn't care to examine.

He took another sip of water, before closing the canteen. "You want to go on?" he asked, narrowing his gaze. "Or do you want to go back?"

Katlin knew she'd had enough—that if she pushed too hard she'd only set herself back. But she didn't want to admit it. A tiny battle went on inside her, then finally, she sighed. "Let's go back. I'm sorry. I know I'm being a bother again."

"The *bother* would come if you'd said you wanted to go on. Instead, you kept your word."

His approval caught her by surprise. Especially

when it sprang from such genuine feeling. As if a person keeping their word was of great importance to him.

God, Honor, Country. Michael had held those principles with deep pride, but she hadn't expected Quint McCabe to feel the same way.

Truly, she knew nothing about him.

Which made her want to learn all she could.

KATLIN RESTED in the afternoon while Quint rode out again. He had a couple of things to see to, he'd said, once more assuring her that what he would be doing was nothing she hadn't seen before, or that she wouldn't see in the future.

She'd gazed speculatively at his trailer after he rode off, but she didn't go inside. If there'd been something to see, she'd have seen it yesterday. And after what she'd sensed from him earlier, she couldn't make herself invade his home again.

After awakening from a long nap, she moved restlessly about the motor home, then went outside to explore the camp. There'd been very little opportunity until now. She had a better look in what he called the tack room, where he kept the many tools of his trade—extra bridles and halters, the saddle she'd been using, saddlebags and blankets, hammers and pliers, horseshoes and other miscellaneous articles. The other storage room had other supplies—from foodstuffs to tools for the light green pickup truck and double horse trailer she found parked out back. She hadn't known the truck and trailer were there, but it stood to reason. No one in such an isolated place would want to rely solely on a horse, and sometimes the horse needed transportation.

She went through the small corral to the larger one to answer Chili's call. She spent a little time stroking the horse's nose and neck, then started back to the motor home.

She was most of the way there when she caught a movement from the corner of her eye. Something long and mottled brown was on the ground, near the motor home's front tire…slithering toward the rear of the vehicle. Right where she'd have stepped if she'd kept going.

She gave a sharp cry of fear, of dismay. She'd never seen a rattlesnake before, not in the wild. And this one was huge! Almost as big around as her arm. Stretched out, it could easily be five or six feet!

It was moving, so it wasn't coiled…and she knew it would have to coil before it struck…at least, she thought she knew that. Everything she'd ever read about rattlers cascaded through her mind to create a jumble. All she really understood was that she wanted to get away.

She started to back up, then turned to run. Straight to Chili. He was the only friend she had at present.

She pounded back the way she'd come, forgetting her remaining aches and pains on a rush of adrenaline. Almost without pause, she latched onto the fence separating the two corrals and climbed to the second rail.

Chili, who'd been standing close to the fence, bolted away. Only when he was at a safe distance did he stop to look at her.

Katlin laughed nervously, realizing that, to him, she'd gone mad. She called to him, speaking softly as she'd seen Quint do, trying to calm the horse as well as herself. Chili ambled back and when at last he stood next to her again, she stroked his cheek to make up for her behavior.

In those few seconds Katlin began to think, not merely react. The snake hadn't raced after her. It couldn't. At most it was probably only a little further along than it had been before.

But she couldn't stop shaking. It had been so big. And what if she hadn't seen it?

She looked at the ground, wondering about a mate. Did rattlers travel in pairs?

Sticks she hadn't seen before looked like snakes. She even saw imaginary snakes where there weren't any sticks!

She felt ridiculous clinging to her perch, but it was the only place she felt safe. And even then, not very.

KATLIN HEARD Jim's metal shoes striking rock before Quint rode into the clearing. She told herself that she should get down, but she couldn't.

Quint rode to the small corral, not seeing her at

first, probably because he didn't expect her to be there.

He leaned over from the saddle to swing open the gate, then as he and Jim moved in, he spotted her.

She might have laughed in other circumstances. He looked so surprised. But then, in other circumstances, she wouldn't have been stranded there.

He urged Jim over to her, frowning. "What's up?" he asked shortly, his gaze moving over her, examining every inch for a cause.

She knew he could tell she wasn't happy about being where she was, and that she'd been there for a while.

"I—I saw a snake," she said, pointing. "A big one...over by the motor home. I almost stepped on it."

His entire demeanor relaxed. "Oh," he grunted. Then he smiled wryly. "Is it still alive?"

"Yes! I didn't hang around to argue. I ran over here. I've been here for...at least an hour!"

"Are you going to get down now?"

"I—"

When she seemed to have difficulty deciding, he urged Jim close and swept her from the rails.

"What are you doing?" she demanded, her feet dangling in the air. His arm was like a tight band around her waist.

"I'm taking you where you want to go," he answered.

Then he had Jim walk them back to the motor home. They stopped a few feet from her door.

Her face flamed from embarrassment and ill humor. Still, she took time for a fearful look around.

"I don't see anything, do you?" he asked, his tone amused.

"It could be under the trailer," she suggested. She wanted to stay angry, but she wanted to be positive the snake was gone more.

"I'll check," he said, then asked before putting her down, "Are you ready?"

"I'm more than ready," she snapped, and soon found herself on the ground.

He slid smoothly out of the saddle with that easy cowboy grace, then had a good look around. He inspected every possible hiding spot within a wide radius of the travel home. "Nothing here," he said at last. "Musta just been passing through."

Katlin instinctively peered around herself. "Aren't you going to search for it? A snake that big has to be dangerous."

"Sure it's dangerous. That's what I told you. You always have to keep a watch out. There are lots of 'em out here."

"You aren't afraid of them?" she demanded.

"Did I say I wasn't?"

"No, but—"

"I just do my best to stay out of their way. If it'd make you feel better, I can find you a big stick to carry around, just in case."

She tried to gauge his seriousness. "How often have you seen one in camp?" she demanded.

"Every once in a while. Not too often, though. That's why I keep the place cleared. Discourages 'em a bit. Also makes them easier to see."

"I'll take the stick," she said firmly.

He touched the crinkled brim of his hat and said, "Whatever you say."

Then he stepped back up into the saddle and rode Jim to the corral. Confirming something Katlin had once read—that a cowboy would rather ride than walk, no matter how short the distance.

KATLIN STAYED IN the motor home, safe from snakes, for the rest of the afternoon. She didn't see Quint outside much either. Which made her display of cowardice easier.

Then he knocked on the door.

When she answered, he stood outside—hatless, chapless, spurless...and looking extremely handsome. He also held a long stick that looked like an old broom handle.

"I've made enough beans and beef for two," he said. "You want to come have some? As a peace offering?" When she hesitated, he smiled. "I brought your stick." He held it out for her approval. "You don't want to go taking on a rattler with this, though. You have to know what you're doing for that. But it's good for rustling around in things and making enough noise to warn the snake you're there. Then he can head off in another direction.''

''You make it sound as if they should be afraid of me,'' Katlin said.

''Maybe it's a mutual thing?''

''A natural balance?''

His smile broadened. ''Now you're gettin' it.''

She smiled faintly. ''Do all cowboys feel like you do? See themselves as protectors of the land and what's on it?''

''Some hate snakes worse than you do.''

''I don't hate them.''

He changed the subject. ''You want some grub?''

''Sure,'' she said.

''Then come over whenever you're ready.''

She watched as he propped the stick beside the door, winked when he was done, then went back to his trailer.

Katlin closed the door. This was starting to get difficult. She needed to be with him, she needed to win him over...but she also needed to stay far away from those pale blue eyes.

CHAPTER EIGHT

THE SUN HAD DROPPED beyond the cliff rim, giving the land a rosy glow, when Katlin walked to Quint's trailer.

She deliberately didn't bring the stick, because she felt she needed to prove a point. To him and to herself. She wanted to show them both that she could overcome her nervousness.

She'd been all over the camp for the past few days and hadn't seen a snake until late this afternoon. There was a good possibility that before she left she wouldn't see another. So she couldn't go around being afraid, or having him think she was afraid.

He'd said only the strong survive in this place. She wanted to show that she was strong.

Quint opened the door as she stepped under the awning. His eyes moved over her in quick appraisal, noting that she held nothing, and that she'd changed to a frillier blouse.

"We can eat inside or outside," he offered. "Your choice."

"Outside," she said.

"Then have a seat. Ah—do you still need a cushion?"

"I'll live dangerously."

"Looks like you already are," he said, before disappearing back inside.

Katlin wasn't sure if he meant he thought she was living dangerously by braving the clearing, or by agreeing to eat dinner with him.

He added a small table between the two metal chairs and brought out a large pot filled with beans and chunks of beef. "What would you like to drink?" he asked. "Soda, beer, water?"

"Soda's fine," she said. "Whatever you have."

While he returned to the trailer, Katlin leaned forward to sniff the pot's aromatic contents. "Mmm," she murmured.

"Hope you like spicy food," he said as he came outside again. "That's got chili and peppers and all kinds of good stuff."

"I do, actually."

"Good. It's the only way I know how to cook."

He dipped into the large pot and filled a bowl for her and one for himself. Then flashing a smile that tickled her toes, he invited, "No need to stand on ceremony. Eat however much you want. There's sourdough bread, too."

The first bite burned her mouth, both from heat and from spiciness, but it tasted wonderful. Far better than the canned meals she'd been preparing for herself.

"It's very good," she said.

He nodded.

They ate in silence for another few minutes, then Katlin sat back, sipped her soda and requested casually, "Tell me about the cowboy who used to live here. Since I'm wearing his things...I'd like to at least know his name."

"Don Simpson. He was here for about five years."

"What happened to him? Why did he leave?"

Quint shrugged. "Got tired of being by himself, I suppose. I heard he married a girl from Mexico."

"Is this place reserved for single cowboys, then? Wives and families are discouraged?"

"No. Just...most women won't put up with being so isolated."

"What about you, if you found a girl?"

"I'm not looking."

She tilted her head. "But, what if you did? Would the Parkers allow you to bring her here to live with you?"

"I don't think they'd care." He sat back, having finished with his meal as well. "What about you? Are you looking? Or are you already claimed?"

Katlin took a moment to answer. "No, I'm not claimed, and I'm not looking, either."

"Why not?"

"I—my work. My work's important to me. And right now—"

"Same here," he broke in.

She met his steady look. "Point taken," she conceded, then tried another approach. "What I'm really asking—being scrupulous to leave out personal preference—is do you think it's better for a man in your situation to be married or single? For any cowboy, really? Is it the kind of life that promotes family?''

''Is this still about the *vanishing* bit?''

She nodded, relieved to be back on the solid ground of her deception. For a while there, she'd been adrift.

''It's not whether a cowboy makes good husband material or not,'' he answered evenly, seemingly ready to take on the broader question. ''Some do, some don't. Just like other men. Obviously, the ones who stick in one place longer are better at it than the ones who pick up and leave because a foreman or an owner looks at 'em funny. The only thing that'll make the cowboy vanish is if people turn their backs on the end result of what he does. Ranchers won't keep ranching if no one buys their beef. If they stop ranching, the cowboy's gone. Just like you said.''

''Even on a big place like this?'' she asked incredulously.

''A place run this way is already unusual. And smaller places often hang on by the skin of their teeth.''

''Mae Parker didn't seem to think—''

''Mae knows.''

''So you're saying the cowboy *is* vanishing?''

''Not is, *could.*''

"What would you do then, *if* he did?" she asked.

"Learn to tap dance?" he suggested facetiously.

"But you said something about oil and gas wells."

"They're not mine."

"No! I meant—"

He smiled. "You seem genuinely concerned. Why should it matter to you whether the Parker Ranch survives or not? Whether the job of a cowboy continues? You're just a reporter, covering a story."

"Yes, but—"

She looked inside herself. Somehow something had shifted. Whether it was because he'd made her dust off her unused MBA to see the ranch as a business or because, as a result of her training, she didn't like to see any type of enterprise with such a long history fail.

Before she could figure it out, he said, "Don't worry. It's not happening yet. Plenty of people still like their hamburgers and steaks. It's just, when they stop—when someone invents some artificial substance that tastes like beef without all the hassle and people can buy it cheap and out of a vending machine—that's when the party will be over."

"There'll always be connoisseurs who'll want the real thing."

"Yes, but will they want it on the hoof, on a ranch, eating grass?"

"Then why do you keep doing it?"

"Because I love it. There's nothing in this world

like getting up early to go out into the pasture to check how everything's doing. You get to watch the sun come up and, if you're out long enough, the sun go down. Watch calves be born and grow. Nothing can beat the satisfaction of gathering cattle on a good horse in the spring and fall, or watching horses run wild and free. There've been times when I'd've given everything I owned to be back—''

He stopped.

Katlin was positive he'd been about to say "here." Just as she was equally positive one of the times he'd have "given everything" to be back at the Parker Ranch was during and shortly after Michael's "accident."

She let the slip pass, knowing that since his guard was already firmly back in place, she would gain nothing by pressing.

"Do you have a TV or radio?" she asked. "Don't you miss hearing the news? Keeping up with current events?"

"I get all the news I need every few weeks when I go in for supplies. There's a radio, but I rarely listen to it."

"What about checking in? What if you got hurt? When you're all by yourself, you're at a disadvantage, aren't you?"

"I don't worry about that."

"But the Parkers...don't they worry?"

"They let me do it how I want. If I didn't show up when I was supposed to, Morgan would probably drive out to see what was going on.'' He stood up. "How about some pound cake to finish up with? My aunt Delores made it—she's Morgan's mother. It's only been in the freezer about a week, so it should be fine. She's a really good cook.''

Katlin looked at the darkness settling around them and knew she should go back. Instead, she nodded and offered, "May I help with the dishes?"

"There's not all that much. I'll get them later.'' He collected the still half-full pot of beans and beef and the much smaller round of bread, and after another trip to clear the rest of the table, he came back outside with coffee and warmed cake, and lit a lantern so they could see to eat it.

Crickets chirped in the bushes and a coyote started yipping in the distance. But Katlin felt safe enough under the awning to actually enjoy the serenade.

After filling their cups, Quint settled in his chair and stretched out his long legs to prop his boots, crossed at the ankle, on a nail keg that must have been set there for expressly that purpose. He did it so easily, he might have done it a thousand times.

"Your aunt made this?'' Katlin asked after her first bite of cake. "It's so rich.''

The golden glow from the lantern highlighted the gold in his hair and deepened the bronze of his skin. "She's always trying to make sure I have enough to eat. She thinks I let myself starve out here.''

Katlin grinned. "If tonight's an example, she doesn't have to worry."

"She doesn't think a table's properly set until she's filled it with enough food to make the legs buckle. She gets worried if you don't ask for seconds."

"My mom's like that," Katlin told him.

"Then you know what I mean. Sometimes I can barely stand straight when I leave their place."

She glanced at him. "Morgan told me his family lives near headquarters. At a place called...Little Springs?"

He nodded. "His mom and dad—my aunt Delores and uncle Dub—have a house there. And Morgan, Christine and their two kids have another. Uncle Dub used to be the foreman before he got hurt and couldn't do the job any more. Then Morgan took over."

"I understand Morgan and Rafe Parker are like brothers?"

"They were raised together, for all intents and purposes. Morgan told me he wasn't sure where he spent more time growing up—Little Springs or headquarters. Rafe's the same."

"Rafe's the ranch manager, right?" She searched for questions to keep him talking.

"He took over from Mae. She did the job after Rafe's father died, then passed the responsibility on to Rafe when he was old enough."

"You know a lot about the place, don't

you...because of your relationship with the Hugheses?''

"I guess I do."

"What about your family? Your mom and dad." It was the type of inquiry anyone would make.

She could feel him tighten up. But to her surprise, he answered.

"My mother lives in Houston with my sister and her family. My dad's dead." He glanced at her. "What about you? Where's your family?"

Katlin stiffened, just as he had. For *him* to ask that of *her!* Still, she knew she had to answer...because he had.

"They're in California."

He whistled softly. "So, you're a valley girl! No wonder you—"

"*Northern* California," she corrected him.

"There's a difference?" was his comeback.

She was beginning to know that special dry quality that entered his voice when he teased her. Also, he'd repeated almost word-for-word her first-day novice question about there being a "difference" between a regular riding horse and a cutting horse. After having witnessed Jim in action, she could understand his irritation at her ignorance.

In the same teasing spirit, she answered with her best valley girl imitation: "Well, like, yeah!"

Quint's smile grew until it broke into full laughter.

Even as she joined in, she was surprised at how

funny he seemed to find her little joke. As if it was the best thing he'd heard in a long time—which possibly it was, considering the length of time he spent alone.

The notion left her with an odd feeling...as if, somehow, it wasn't appropriate for a person of such obvious intelligence and droll sense of humor to have so successfully hidden himself away from the world.

"Touché," he murmured, still chuckling. Then he noticed her empty coffee cup. "Would you like some more of that?"

Katlin stared at the cup she didn't remember drinking from and shook her head as she stood up. "No, I—I really need to be going. Five-thirty will come early, for both of us."

"We can put it off a little, if you like," he offered, uncrossing his boots to stand up as well. "Nothing says we *have* to be out before sunrise."

She shook her head. "No. I've already interfered with your schedule enough. Five-thirty is fine."

She glanced at him and then away again.

She didn't want to feel anything. She had to stay focused. She couldn't let his attractiveness undermine the fact that he remained her quarry. She was here, putting herself through this, for a reason. For Michael...*Michael!* She all but spoke his name out loud, using it as a talisman, to keep from—

She hadn't realized that she'd lifted her gaze again until, transfixed, she watched the effect her hesitation to leave had on Quint. He'd been standing, free and easy, a responsible dinner host, even if they were in the back of beyond, until something electric triggered in the air between them. His stillness became infectious. Katlin couldn't move or breathe. Then he reached for her—touching her cheek, lifting her chin. And their lips met.

Messages flashed back and forth. Silent messages that bypassed conscious thought. Katlin knew she should pull away, but couldn't.

The prolonged kiss was intense, exciting and at the same time...so very right!

For a few seconds the intimacy deepened, with the promise of more to come, then he pulled back.

Katlin still couldn't move. His fingers continued to support her chin; her mouth still tingled and throbbed from the feel of his.

In the golden lamplight, his pale eyes smiled at her and she wanted the moment never to end.

"That was nice," he said, his voice soft, husky. "But this is probably where we should leave it for now...don't you think?"

The decision was in her hands. He was leaving it up to her.

Sanity returned in a rush. Katlin jerked her chin to the side and made herself step away from him.

"I'll take that as a...yes?" he murmured, smiling.

She stared at him with dazed eyes.

"Would you like me to walk you back to your trailer?" he asked.

"No," she said, her voice strained.

"You're not afraid of snakes any more?"

"Not the ones on the ground."

He chuckled at her flippant reply. "I hope you're not thinking I'm a snake."

"I honestly don't know what I think," she admitted. Snake...temptation—*if the shoe fit*.... She shook her head.

"Don't worry about it," he said soothingly. "Nothing happened. And what did wasn't so bad."

She looked toward the motor home, where she'd had enough presence of mind earlier to leave on a light. "I—I have to go. Thanks for dinner. It was...delicious."

"Yes," he agreed, "it was."

Only he wasn't referring to their dinner. And truth to tell—once she'd regained the safety of the motor home and could admit such a thing—Katlin wasn't sure that she had been either.

A ROLLING CRACK of thunder awakened Katlin the next morning, better than any alarm clock. It was soon followed by loud splats as raindrops hit the motor home's roof and the surrounding ground. The heavy rain came suddenly, and didn't let up even after the first half hour.

Katlin switched on a light to chase away the gloom. There was no chance of going back to sleep, even though she'd tossed and turned for a good portion of the night, unable to settle.

She propped a second pillow behind her head after choosing one of the paperbacks she'd brought for just such an occasion.

He wouldn't be going out in weather like this, surely. Was he doing the same thing she was? His large selection of books bore silent witness to the probability. Her thoughts moved to a visual picture of him in bed. She doubted that, even though it was all she'd ever seen him in, he slept in his jeans and long-sleeved shirt....

She forced the errant thought away and concentrated on the initial paragraph of the novel. She'd yet to reach the end of the first line when someone—Quint—rapped on her door.

Abandoning the book, she slipped her robe over her gown and pulled it close around her as she opened the door.

He stood outside, holding a slicker over his head to ward off most of the rain, though some droplets found their way onto his bare chest, making the light sprinkling of darker hair glisten. He wore jeans and a shirt, but the shirt wasn't fastened. Katlin's heart rate quickened to spite her.

"Just checking to see how you're making out," he said, raising his voice to be heard.

"I'm fine," she answered. "Are the horses—" She'd been going to ask if they were fine, too, when she remembered that neither of them was accustomed to being cosseted.

"I just fed 'em. They're snug as can be in their shed."

She smiled. Then she realized that he was getting wetter the longer he stood talking to her. "Would you like to come in? I—"

He shook his head "No. Better not."

As his pale eyes flitted over her, she tightened her grip on the robe's lapels. She hadn't thought to give him the impression that she *wanted* him to come in. She hadn't meant—

Thunder clapped above them, then reverberated through the hills and canyons—a heavenly reminder to Katlin not to forget what she was doing. She gave him a quick, tight smile and swung the door closed until only a narrow crack remained. The impression she gave might be that she was afraid of thunder, but she didn't care.

"We'll see how long this keeps up," he said. "But we'll probably stick close to camp today." He frowned. "Is something wrong?"

She shook her head. "No, I just—" She glanced up at the sky and his frown lightened.

"Worst will probably be over soon," he said. "Don't have to worry about flooding. We're in a high spot here, so fast runoff won't be a problem."

"Okay."

He stood under his slicker for another moment, studying what he could see of her. Then he shook his head slightly, muttered a quick, "See you later," and darted back to his trailer.

Katlin closed the door and turned to lean back against it. She didn't know what was wrong with her! Why did she keep reacting that way? Why could one look from those blue eyes of his unsettle her so badly?

QUINT WAS GOOD at controlling his instincts, first because his father had expected it, then because the Army did. He'd always prided himself on the strength of his discipline. But with her? He was seriously starting to question himself. It was all he could do to refuse her offer to come in out of the rain.

Mae trusted him. She'd sent Katlin Carter to Big Spur for that very reason. But he was only a man. When she stood there looking so fresh and beautiful, with her hair mussed and the fragrance of sweet bathsoap surrounding her, in a soft silk gown that peeped out from beneath the robe she was attempting to hold around herself—it was more than he could handle.

He paced back and forth across the living room floor. Damn the rain! He needed to work. He needed to keep his mind occupied, so he wouldn't think about her.

Was he seriously entertaining the possibility of a long-term relationship between them? Or was he thinking more along the lines of something temporary, until she gathered all the material she needed and left?

Once, he would have settled for the latter, taking what he could get, as would most unattached males. He'd done his share of that kind of thing in his younger brasher days—when his life's path had seemed so solidly set, when willing women were easy to find and when following established military procedures always ensured continuing success.

He dropped into the worn recliner and rubbed the center of his forehead. Damn the rain!

It had been raining the night they'd lifted off for Manzant....

Quint hadn't particularly liked the operation from the beginning. The foray into the tiny unsettled Caribbean republic had had a certain smell and wasn't what *he* did. But Colonel Raymond Tucker had called him into his office and made a special request. The same Colonel Tucker Quint had known all his life.

"We have a man inside we need to get out," Colonel Tucker had told him, biting down on the stub of his unlit cigar.

"Why tell me?" Quint had protested. "I'm not—"

"Because you're the man Damon Surette wants. Remember him? He was part of that 'special' group you trained two years ago."

Quint nodded. He remembered the mercenary very well. Surette wasn't someone you wanted to turn your back on. An ideologue to the point of fanaticism, he was also a quick learner, who too often bragged of the number of people he'd killed.

"He's worked his way to the head of one of the rebel forces in Manzant," the Colonel went on. "The government there has recently arrested a U.S. citizen for spying. Surette broke him out. Now he wants to give him to us."

Quint frowned. "Who is this guy?"

"A U.S. citizen. That's all you need to know."

"This sounds like something for the Rangers or Delta Force. Not me."

"You're it. Surette's nervous. Thinks everyone's out to get him. He specifically asked for you."

Quint's frown deepened. "We weren't all that friendly. In fact—"

"He remembers you. That's all that matters." The Colonel paused. "This isn't something the powers that be want spread around. In fact, the fewer people who know about it, the better. A quick in-and-out, tonight. Report to Orion Field at thirteen-hundred hours. You'll be briefed."

Quint had saluted smartly, then left the office.

He knew he wasn't getting the full story, but his was not to reason why. He'd been given an order to carry out.

Two hours later he was on the hot tarmac and Colonel Tucker himself filled him in as they walked to the jet that would take him to the base on the east coast where he was to meet the rest of his crew— three members of an elite Army force, who were to act as mission bodyguards, and the crack helicopter unit that would fly them safely in and out. They were all to load into transport, the helicopter included, and fly to the base closest to their objective. From there the team would leave for Manzant.

"Surette's jumping," Colonel Tucker had said. "Things are heating up and he doesn't want to lose his bargaining chip. And our 'powers' are getting excited, too. So we have to do this flast—fast," he corrected. "This…operation. No one's to…know." He shook his head and blinked several times.

When Quint reacted with concern, the Colonel behaved as if there was nothing to worry about. He rubbed his arm and flexed his fingers. "Just a little twinge, son. Almost everyone past sixty gets them on occasion." Then he'd slapped Quint on the back. "Something whippersnappers like you don't have to worry about for a long time yet. Drop by my office when you get back. Good luck."

Quint had met the men who would, in effect, be under his command and talked briefly with them during the flight south. The three bodyguards were young and strong and charged for the mission. The helicopter crew bracketed his age—late twenties to mid-thirties.

When they'd arrived at their final base of operation, it was raining. Hard, blowing rain that changed to drizzle just before they had to launch.

The darkness was nothing to the pilots who were

wearing night-vision devices. They were experts at flying in conditions that were less than perfect.

Quint was dressed like the others—flak vest over dark camouflage fatigues and a helmet. He carried an automatic weapon as well. The entire operation had been carefully planned, but when entering an area as unstable as Manzant anything could happen. Even in the best of times, it was difficult to tell who your friends were.

The rotors roared overhead as the helicopter cut through the damp air. Then a quick circle and they were down.

The blades continued turning, as Quint and the three guards quickly exited the chopper and headed through the heavy mist to the meeting point.

All was still going well when they came upon a group of silent men. Someone said Quint's name and after he gave a clipped reply, a handsome man with sharp eyes and sharp features—Damon Surette—broke away from the rest.

He'd been frowning fiercely, but had just started to smile, when they took fire. Bullets whizzed by, snapping loudly, like the crack of a branch or sticks. Men yelled, yowled, swore—some fell. The bodyguards, as well as most of the waiting men, ducked and returned fire.

Damon Surette dragged a man forward. A rather nondescript man in a filthy, rumpled suit, who looked nearly frightened out of his mind. "Here! Take him! I hand him over! Tell your president I have kept my promise. Now he is to remember his! Better than he remembered his last one!''

Then the groups dispersed. The rebels back into the jungle; the bodyguards, Quint and their charge, back toward the helicopter. Quint returned fire as he ran, all the while pushing the frightened man ahead of him.

One of the guards cried out and went down. A bad hit to his neck. His buddies grabbed him and dragged him along with them, even as they continued to spray bullets to the rear.

The helicopter came into sight. The crew chief hung out the door, frantically waving them in. They covered the distance as fast as they could.

A second guard was hit just as he was about to leap on board. Quint tossed their charge into the chopper, then helped the crew chief pull the injured man inside. Both of them were reaching for the second injured guard, when the crew chief took a bullet to the middle of his forehead. The man looked surprised, grunted and collapsed.

Pandemonium ruled inside the helicopter as Quint and the last guard rolled the remaining man inside and jumped in themselves as the chopper lifted. Quint felt the ground disappear from beneath his feet before he was even fully in.

The next minutes were crammed with the actions of trying to save dying men. Those unharmed did everything they could...and still the three who had been hit didn't make it.

Anger, frustration, tears. From the helicopter crew, from the lone remaining guard. Even from Quint, who hadn't known any of these men when he'd had breakfast that morning.

Quint drew an uneven breath, his fingers still pressing against his forehead as he sat in the worn recliner.

Soldiers accustomed to combat became hardened to the death of friends and strangers. They had to. They had little other choice. Quint knew he'd be haunted by these deaths for the rest of his life.

And their loss was made even more personal by what had followed.

The operation had been a screwup. Conceived in too much of a rush, with too many hands and agencies in the pot. The signal for a diversion that Surette had relied on for a safe turnover had not been given. The Manzant government troops, with nothing to distract them, had rushed to where the helicopter had been heard landing, resulting in the firefight. And the person who was supposed to have supplied the highly secret radio burst to alert Surette's rebels to begin the diversion, turned out to be Quint.

This detail came out several days later. Days Quint had spent at the hospital with Agnes Tucker as she waited to learn whether her husband would survive the massive stroke he'd suffered the morning after the disastrous mission.

Agnes and Raymond had no children and had always considered Quint and his older sister, Nina, as substitutes. Though they were not blood relations, Quint and Nina had always termed them "aunt" and "uncle."

Divergent postings had almost always kept the families apart, but a special bond held them together. When Raymond Tucker had been a shavetailed lieutenant straight out of West Point, he'd been shipped off to the war in Korea. Charlie McCabe had already been there for six months functioning proudly as a new Sergeant. The story, as Quint had heard it all his life, was that the first thing Lieutenant Tucker tried to do was get himself killed, and it had been Charlie McCabe who'd saved his "shiny pink ass." Raymond had never forgotten. His rise in the ranks didn't put a strain on the friendship, and Charlie, a dyed-in-the-wool enlisted man, had allowed that— just possibly—there was one Army officer who was all right.

Raymond sank into a world of his own after the stroke. Agnes and Quint sat by his bed, but he didn't know it. Agnes had confided that he'd been feeling unwell for the past month, but—being a proud and fiercely stubborn man—he'd been trying to hang on until the first week in February when he planned to retire.

Those first few days, following the mission, could have come from the pages of a horror novel as far as Quint was concerned. The hospital had decorated for Christmas, but Quint could feel no cheer.

He'd gotten wind that the brass was looking for

someone to hang out to dry...in a quiet way, because they'd rather the whole operation disappeared from memory. They'd gotten their suited-man back, Damon Surette must have received whatever it was he wanted—all was well, except for three dead soldiers. And that couldn't be left alone. In case anyone ever learned of it, they wanted to have some action to point to, to show that they'd dealt severely with the person responsible.

Quint knew he'd never been given instructions to radio in to start the diversion. If he'd been supposed to do it...Colonel Tucker was the person who should have told him.

Colonel Tucker, who'd served his country with honor and valor for over forty years and been decorated in two major wars.

Colonel Tucker, battling an illness at the time of briefing Quint for his mission.

Colonel Tucker, now a virtual vegetable in his hospital bed, with a devoted wife at his side.

Colonel Tucker who had quietly watched out for Charlie McCabe and his family for so many years, and when Charlie was so terribly ill himself, had made sure his friend had had the best available treatment in the best military hospital, as well as ensuring that Quint's mother Heddy and any family member could stay nearby during their vigil.

The only person to know that Quint hadn't been given the order was in that bed.

Quint, standing alone beside him while Agnes had

gone for coffee, squeezed the older man's unresponsive hand, and made the only decision he could live with.

He took the responsibility on himself.

CHAPTER NINE

THE STORM EVENTUALLY STOPPED but a light rain continued to fall until shortly before noon. When at last the sun broke through, Katlin looked up from the book she'd been reading, stretched and put it aside. She had no idea what the rest of the day would bring, but a morning lost in a fictional world had been a pleasant release.

She went to a side window and peeked outside. Freshly washed, the camp looked brighter, more alive. She could see Chili and Jim moving around in the far corral, trotting energetically. Birds chirped, happy the storm had passed. But of Quint, she saw nothing. His trailer had a closed-off feel.

She opened all her windows and let the slight breeze waft through. Then she went back to her book. He would come out when he was ready.

Over the next hour she munched a sandwich as she continued to read, and leisurely drank a cup of tea. It had been a long time since she'd been able to do as she wanted. She hadn't spent what could be termed a free day since the single day of Christmas vacation she'd shared with her parents before they'd learned of Michael's death. Since then, her life had not been her own. Not that she minded! she quickly thought. Just—for this one moment—it felt a long time.

She took a deep breath, then released it hastily at the sound of an approaching motor. She hurried to the window in time to see a ranch pickup pull to a stop at the end of the road.

As she watched, Morgan Hughes stepped out from behind the wheel, while a pretty woman with shoulder-length chestnut hair exited from the passenger door.

Katlin hurried to check her appearance. She'd had a shower and dressed not long before, but she wanted to project a crisply professional image. The visit, in all likelihood, was at Mae Parker's instigation.

By the time she'd made the needed repairs, Quint had appeared to greet the newcomers. He shook Morgan's hand then hugged the woman as she kissed his cheek. A moment later everyone glanced toward the motor home and Katlin knew she had to join them.

She smiled a bright friendly smile and stepped outdoors.

"There she is," Morgan said in salutation. "Miss Carter." He offered her his hand.

"Katlin, please."

Her eyes made a quick survey of the trio. Morgan Hughes looked exactly as he had the first day she'd met him, only with the coat of dust removed. The woman was prettier than Katlin had thought at first. Quint seemed strained, distant.

Katlin frowned. The visitors hadn't been there long enough to have imparted bad news, and the last time she'd seen him he'd been his usual self…at least, what she knew of his usual self.

"I'm Christine Hughes, Morgan's wife," the woman introduced herself, smiling. Her hazel eyes were quick, intelligent, curious. They probed without being intrusive.

"Hello," Katlin said.

"What brings you folks out here?" Quint asked, cordial but direct.

Morgan's grin was easy. "Christine wanted to get out of the house for a while, so I suggested a little drive. She was also burnin' up to meet Miss Carter, here. Ah…Katlin," he corrected. "Mom would have come, too, but Beth's been under the weather with a cold the past few days, and she volunteered to stay with her so Christine could have a break."

"Beth's your daughter?" Katlin said, responding as expected.

"One of them—" Christine smiled "—our youngest. She's three. Doesn't deal well with being sick. She's like her daddy in that regard…she takes it as a personal affront."

"Hey, don't blame it all on me!" Morgan defended himself. "You get a little testy, too, when you're not well."

"*I* don't act like a bear."

"A teddy bear?" he teased.

Christine giggled as the four of them moved toward the shade of the awning. The pair had to have been married for some time, yet from their relaxed and easy way, Katlin could tell the love they originally had for each other remained strong.

Katlin glanced at Quint as she sat in one of the chairs and Christine took the other. Standing off to one side, he still had a restless quality to him. Her impression was that the last thing he wanted at that moment was company.

Morgan must have sensed the same thing, because after a little strained small talk about the change in weather, he proposed, "How about you and me leavin' the ladies to it for a while, Quint? They can get to know one another, while we talk cattle."

"Sounds good," Quint said. His gaze, flicking over Katlin, was as schooled as his expression. "Kitchen's yours to do with what you want, ladies…if you want coffee or something." Then he turned away.

Morgan squeezed his wife's shoulder before following.

The two women watched them go. They moved to the corral as if drawn by a magnet, where each hooked a boot heel on the lower rail and folded their arms comfortably across the top.

Christine laughed lightly, her gaze warm. "A matched pair," she murmured. "I've seen a photograph of their grandfather. You can certainly tell where they get their looks. Down to the way they're standing now.''

''Their grandfather was a cowboy?'' Katlin asked, suddenly realizing Christine could be a valuable source of information.

''He owned a place in Central Texas. Not big by Parker Ranch standards, but big enough. Hit on bad times, though, and ended up selling. Delores, Morgan's mother, told me it broke his heart. Happened back when she and her sister Heddy—that's Quint's mother—were girls. He died a short time after.''

''That's terrible.''

''Yes,'' Christine agreed. Interest sparked in her eyes. ''How are you and Quint getting on? Are you finding any useful information for your article?''

''Quite a bit,'' Katlin answered easily.

''And Quint? He's not exactly the easiest person in the world to get to know, but when you do, he's pretty special. Then again—'' she grinned ''—I'm family and I'm prejudiced.''

''Oh, we're fine,'' Katlin replied offhandedly. ''He considers my being here a pain, but he's putting up with it.''

Christine laughed, then glanced around. ''I don't know how he's lived out here on his own for so long. But I guess—'' She stopped.

''What?'' Katlin prompted.

''He must have his reasons.''

''Are you telling me he's not naturally a recluse?''

Christine tilted her head. "You know, I never considered that...but I suppose it could look that way. No, he's not a recluse. He doesn't hate other people. Did you really think that?"

Katlin shrugged. "It's just...a possibility."

"He hasn't always been a cowboy. He's been out in the world."

"Doing what?"

Christine moved uncomfortably. "Just...things. Ordinary things."

Katlin smiled to keep the other woman friendly, even as she pushed the envelope of inquiry a little further. "He's certainly good at giving orders. Do this...don't do that."

"Aren't most men?" Christine kidded, refusing to be drawn.

Katlin changed course. "Do you have a photo of your baby?"

"Do I ever! Wait here." She went to the pickup, took something from the glove box and came back, carrying a small thin photo album. "Morgan keeps this with him all the time. Here," she said, pointing. "This is Beth. Looks like her daddy, doesn't she?"

Katlin studied the photo of a curly-haired little cherub. She had a mass of thick blond hair and the same smile as her father.

"She does," Katlin agreed, "but there's something else...."

"That's the Parker in her coming out. She can be a fierce little thing sometimes."

"The *Parker?*"

"The line comes through me. I didn't know I was a Parker until I was grown." She flipped a page. "And this is my daughter Erin. She's Morgan's, too, since he adopted her."

Katlin gazed at the serious face of the near-adult woman in the photo, then at the young mother, sitting across from her, who looked barely in her thirties. "She's your daughter? But you're not old enough to have— Are you?"

"Everyone says that." Christine smiled. "I had her when I was very young. Actually, the same age Erin is now. She's seventeen."

"My goodness."

Christine flipped through the two remaining pages. "This is Dub and Delores. And their other son, Russell, and his family. And that's it. That's the Hugheses."

"A nice looking family."

"A nice family, which is more important."

"Have you and Morgan been married long?"

"Almost nine years." She suddenly remembered something. "Oh! Before I forget…Gwen said to tell you hello. You really made an impression there. Her mom, Harriet, has been trying to get her to focus on a particular interest for her future. Now, Gwen's told her she's thinking of going into journalism, like you."

The information made Katlin uncomfortable.

"She thinks what you do is very glamorous," Christine continued.

"It's—I'm just gathering information."

"She'll probably change her mind a dozen times before she heads off to college. But if it sticks and that's what she ends up doing, the rest of you are going to have to watch out."

"She's fierce, too?"

"All the Parkers are."

A few seconds passed, then Katlin said, "Speaking of Parkers. Are you really here to get out of the house? Or is it because Mae Parker asked you to come check up on things—me, mainly?"

"She said you were smart."

"What else did she say?"

"That's it. Yes, she did ask us to stop by...but the other part is right, too. It's not fun being cooped up with a cranky three-year-old."

"What will you tell Mae when you see her?"

"That neither of you seems any the worse for wear. Quint's quiet, but he gets that way on occasion. Never when he comes to visit us, but Morgan says—" She stopped.

"What?" Katlin encouraged, seemingly without guile, trying not to act as vitally interested as she really was.

"Well, the longest we ever see him at Little Springs is overnight, and getting him to agree to that is rare. Morgan sees him during roundups, though. Those usually take about a month, twice a year. He says Quint goes all quiet sometimes. Can hardly get a word out of him for a day or two. Does his job, but retreats into himself. It's best to let him be then, Morgan says. Might be a good idea for you to do the same.''

''Up to now, he's been a perfect gentleman,'' Katlin prevaricated.

''An officer and a—'' Again Christine stopped short, obviously concerned that she'd said too much.

Katlin retained her guileless expression, as if having heard nothing untoward.

When she started to talk about other things, the woman slowly relaxed.

A DARK CLOUD hung over Quint even after the passage of the storm. Any time he let himself remember what had happened three years ago, it took hours— sometimes days—to pull himself back together again. To reconcile his life to the way it was, not to the way it might have been.

Three men had died. He was one of the lucky ones. He, at least, had been given time to *have* a life, even if that included denouncement and disgrace.

He'd followed a path chosen by his own free will. And he'd choose it again in a heartbeat.

Morgan tapped his elbow. ''You listenin'?''

''Ah…sure…yeah,'' Quint murmured.

''No, you're not. I just asked what you thought about what Mae said.''

"Mae?" Quint asked blankly.

His cousin sighed. "About that magazine lady. Mae told me to tell you to tread lightly with her."

"What did she mean by that?" Quint frowned.

"That's what I was askin' you."

Quint shrugged.

Morgan looked over his shoulder at the two women sitting under the awning. "Too bad she doesn't have a huge wart on her nose and rotten teeth. How's it goin' in that regard? The day I brought her out here, I thought your eyes were going to pop out of your head. She's a pretty little thing. Kinda soft lookin'."

"I took her out before sunup Wednesday morning. Didn't come back until after four. Just about killed her, but she didn't make a peep. She might look soft, but she's not."

"Hmm." After a moment he said, "Christine seems to like her."

Quint chanced a quick look. "Yeah."

"You goin' out this afternoon later?"

"May."

"Well, we won't be hangin' around long. Christine packed a picnic lunch and we thought we'd eat it over by Drover's Bluff. Don't get too many chances to be on our own, so we have to take advantage."

Quint nodded.

When it became apparent Quint wasn't going to add to the conversation, Morgan said, "Well, if I can tear Christine away, we'll be goin'. Any message you want me to pass along back at headquarters?''

''Nope.''

Morgan smiled. ''At least we don't have to worry about you talkin' her ear off. She'll be lucky if she gets half a page out of you, much less an entire article.''

Morgan collected Christine, and after goodbyes, Quint stood with Katlin to wave them off.

As soon as they were on their own again, Quint muttered, ''Gotta see to the horses,'' and left her standing where she was.

KATLIN SIGHED with dissatisfaction as she watched him walk away. She hadn't been able to make great use of her time alone with Christine Hughes. The woman had been friendly, told her a few things and made vague reference to others, but she'd given her nothing of true importance.

An officer and a gentleman... Katlin already knew he'd attained the rank of Captain. *Periods where he was quiet...* she knew about that as well, from her own experience.

He seemed even more withdrawn this afternoon, though.

Did he think about the accident? Did bad memories cause his withdrawal? Three men had died. That was enough to bring distress to anyone. Particularly if, as his near-immediate resignation indicated, he was the person responsible for—

She couldn't complete the thought. She wanted only cold hard fact. She would not let herself visit on him what the Army officer had intimated about Michael. She wanted to hear Quint's side of the story.

Katlin went back to the motor home and reclaimed the book she'd been reading earlier, but she couldn't keep her mind on it.

Why was she so unwilling to lay the blame on Quint McCabe for what had happened? For the altruistic reason she'd come up with before, or was it something else? Because she sensed that, ever so slightly, she might be starting to fall in love with him?

The possibility left her gasping.

No! Not love. Not with him. *It couldn't be!* There was Michael to consider. Her plan. Her parents. The years of her life she'd given. There was also the short time involved…she still barely knew him! It was attraction. Only attraction. Not love. Not even the littlest, tiniest glimmer!

He knocked on her door. The devil with blue eyes. Oh, God!

"Yes?" she called, her throat so tight the word was almost a croak.

"I'm tired of sitting around," he called. "You want to ride?"

Katlin thought of herself continuing to stew in the

motor home, debating what she felt...or didn't feel. Going out for a ride with him wasn't the solution she'd have seized upon ordinarily, but it was the better of her two choices. "Um...yes. Yes, I do."

"Why won't you open the door?" he demanded.

"Because I'm changing. I'll—I'll be ready in a couple of minutes." She paused. "Should I bring a sandwich?"

"Guess it wouldn't hurt."

"Are you bringing one?" she asked.

"Yeah, I guess."

Oh, this was going to be fun. He didn't want to talk. She didn't want to talk. "Ah—okay. I'll bring one."

There was another long pause. For a second she thought he'd left, but just as she was about to whip off her nicer blouse and slip into a T-shirt, he said, "I'll be over at the corral."

"Okay."

"Okay," he repeated. Then, finally, she heard his boots scrunch the rocky ground as he walked away.

THEIR CONVERSATION was minimal, as Katlin expected. A word here or there, before she fell into place behind him and they rode into an area similar to where they'd been the first day. Her riding skills had improved greatly, though. She was able to relax more in the saddle, not hold herself so tense or stiff. As a result, she didn't hurt nearly as much.

It felt good to be covering ground on a horse,

which surprised her. She'd grown up seeing the occasional horse pastured in the summer-gold, winter-green fields in certain quarters of the Bay Area, but she'd never fantasized about riding one.

"You doing okay?" Quint turned to ask.

"Yes, fine," she answered and this time she meant it.

They came upon a section of fence that needed repair and Katlin watched as he repeated his previous action, only this time having to patch the top two wires that had been broken.

She kept a cautious eye for snakes. She even saw one sunning itself on a rock, but the effect on her wasn't the same. She took note of it, as did Quint, but she didn't panic.

For a time they rode along the fence banked sporadically with tumbleweeds. The rain had freshened everything here, too. She could almost feel the grass growing.

The normal dusty haze had been washed away and when they came to the edge of a plateau, Katlin was given her first panoramic view across a wide rugged valley to the jagged peaks beyond. In the crystalline air the long row of mountains looked close enough to touch, but since this was one of the eighty-mile vistas Quint had told her about, all she could do was marvel at the beauty.

Katlin felt Quint's eyes on her, as if he wanted to gauge the impact. The horses, side-by-side, were as quiet as their riders.

The longer Katlin gazed at the breathtaking scene, the quieter her mind became. A peace like none she'd ever known before settled over her. The timelessness of the land assuaged all worry.

"You feel it, too," Quint stated softly.

She could sense the same peace in him. His restlessness had disappeared. "Yes," she breathed.

"I like to come here when things start to get me down. It always helps."

"Yes," she breathed again.

He looked at her for a long time, then said, "Let's move on."

Katlin nodded and they turned the horses away from the rim.

HER SENSE OF PEACE endured as, a short time later, they stopped to eat their sandwiches. They barely spoke, but Katlin no longer felt cut off.

She watched Quint as he again checked the saddle rigging prior to their starting off.

He was very pleasing to the eye—long and lithe, strong without being bulky, with his burnished skin and fair hair. A man's man in a man's world, yet one any woman would appreciate. It was easy to see why she responded to him.

She pulled her gaze away. She didn't want to think about that right now.

Or to wonder what he must have looked like in uniform.

Or what assignment had resulted in his path and Michael's crossing.

She fiddled with her empty water bottle, then stood up, the feeling of peace ebbing when she thought about her brother.

Quint glanced at her as she stowed the bottle in Chili's saddlebag. "You seem to be holding up better this time."

"I am," she said. "I'm actually enjoying this."

"Enough to quit your job and come work on a ranch?" He teased.

"My job can be done anywhere. That's what's so nice about it."

"How'd you come to be doing this? Did you just decide one day you wanted to write for a magazine?"

Questions, from him. His mood was again changing.

"I got lucky," she quipped. The generality, she'd found, satisfied most inquiries. It answered, without really explaining a thing.

"Did you study journalism in school?" he persisted.

She fell back on the made-up résumé she'd used when applying for the researcher's job at *Eyes On Texas* magazine. "I'm an English major."

He cocked his head. "If you can write, you can write…right?"

She smiled at his play on words. "Something like that."

"Why the *Vanishing Texas Cowboy?*"

She couldn't give him the same answer she'd given Mae. He was exploring deeper. "A friend suggested it. I thought it sounded interesting."

"So here you are."

She shrugged at happenstance.

"Was this a good friend?" he asked.

Katlin saw where he was going. To head him off, she said, "Yes, she is. She's like a sister." Then, quickly, she asked, "What about you? How did you come to be doing this?"

Her use of his words made rebuff difficult. Still, he found a way to delay. "Let's get started. We don't want to lose daylight."

They mounted and rode side-by-side, since the area wasn't as brushy and the trail allowed it.

"Is what I say going to turn up in your article?" he asked.

"Not if you object."

"Then why do you need to know?"

"I'm curious, remember?"

That was the wrong thing to say. She could feel him close up when reminded of her snooping. She tried to make amends. "I don't *need* to know. If you don't want to tell me, you don't have to. It's not important. I—I like you, that's all. I was just…curious."

He didn't say anything for a moment, then answered quietly, "When I was fourteen, I came to live with Aunt Delores and Uncle Dub for a few years. I had to learn to ride—learn a lot of things, really. Uncle Dub took me out with him, so I earned my spurs the hard way.'' He paused, remembering. ''I loved it, once I got used to it.''

''The Parkers let you work on the ranch?''

''After school, during roundups and in summers. I graduated from Del Norte High School.''

''Then you came to work here full time?''

''I did something else for a while...then I came back.''

Katlin felt a pang of anticipation. One more question and she could hit paydirt! But was this the right moment to delve deeper? She'd made a good deal of headway. He'd actually referred to his time in the Army. But his reference had been oblique. He continued to keep that part of his past hidden. If she blundered in too soon, all could be lost.

She licked her lips. ''What...did your aunt and uncle think of you coming back? They must have been very happy to see you.'' Not a great follow-up, but adequate and safe.

He took several moments to reply. The lag was enough to draw her gaze. She was surprised at the sadness she saw etched in his features.

''They were happy to see me,'' he replied, without emotion.

Katlin was searching for something more to say, when Quint suddenly pulled up. She instinctively copied his action, then looked where he looked.

When they'd crested the hill, they'd inadvertently

disturbed a bull. The massive animal stood about forty yards away, his muscles tight, his ears turned. All his attention was directed at them.

Then, tensing even more, he pierced the air with loud bellow after bellow.

CHAPTER TEN

KATLIN WENT RIGID with fear as she looked at the angry bull, but she saw that Quint, though intent, remained calm.

The bulk of the bull's splendidly proportioned body was dark red, with contrasting white face, neck and belly. His thick curved horns, cut on the tips, still had plenty of fight in them. He brandished them like weapons as he scraped the ground, lofting dirt and bits of grass over his shoulders. Then a rumbling growl came from deep inside him. A challenge.

Judging by how fast a cow could run, Katlin wondered if they'd be like pennies left flat on the railroad track after this locomotive charged through.

"Nice and easy now, do what I do," Quint instructed quietly. Then, as if nothing was happening across the way, he turned Jim to move slowly back down the slope. Katlin and Chili did the same.

Her face must have been totally devoid of color when, finally, Quint stopped their slow retreat. Her heart jackhammered in her chest, though it felt lodged in her throat. Her breaths were quick, uneven. "He—" she started to say and choked. "Were we almost killed back there?"

"Are you going to fall out of the saddle?"

"No, I—"

"You want to get down?"

She looked over her shoulder at the none-too-distant hill crest and shook her head, even though there was no sign of the aggrieved bull.

Quint smiled with mild amusement. "No, we weren't going to be killed. All we did was excite him a little bit. We startled him. He reacted like any range bull would when he thought his territory was being invaded. If he hadn't, I'd be worried about him."

"So he wasn't going to charge us?"

"He'd've figured out eventually that we're not competition."

"He's so big!"

"Couple of thousand pounds. He's also boss bull. He and the other bulls fought it out when they were first turned into this pasture last spring."

"There's more of them?" A renewed note of fear was in Katlin's voice as she took another quick survey around them.

"Approximately one bull for every fifteen or sixteen cows."

"They've been here all this time?"

"Won't be taken to their winter pasture until the fall roundup. That's when the real fun begins. Ground shakes when all the bulls from the different divisions are put together in one big place. They find out real quick who can whip who."

"So that bull might not be boss bull any more?"

"Not of the winter pasture. Then again, maybe he will. Just depends on how strong and tough he is."

Quint was talking so matter-of-factly about something that, to Katlin, was as awesome as the animal they'd just encountered. When he eased them back into motion again, she fell into place alongside him…as effortlessly as if she'd been doing it forever, her fear once again lessening.

"Why so many bulls?" she asked, without really thinking it through.

He glanced at her. "How do you think calves get here?"

Her cheeks pinkened. "No, I mean—one for fifteen."

"It's usually one for twenty in flat land, but this is rough country and the cows can hide better. The more bulls there are to find 'em, the more cows get pregnant. These bulls mate about four or five times a day. They take their jobs pretty seriously, too."

The thought of such a huge bull— Katlin shook her head, blinking.

Quint chuckled. "Boggles the mind, hmm? I've seen a boss bull knock another bull away before he's hardly had a chance to get started. Seems greedy, but it's really just nature trying to make the best match. Keep the strongest genes going."

"So most of the calves are from the boss bull?"

"He can only turn his attention to one cow at a time. The others take care of their business when he's not around, or when he's already preoccupied. Usually they have their own group of cows. Genes get spread. They're all good bulls. Come from superior lineage. The Parkers don't keep ones that aren't.''

They rode on. Katlin quiet; Quint doing his job. He checked a calf, put medicine in its eyes, then, after riding back to her, continued the previous conversation as if he'd just spoken.

''Just like they work to keep cows that calve easily—the cows that don't need any outside help—which is the goal of most cowmen. They're also big on conformity, keeping a uniform appearance to the herd—good confirmation, color. You'll notice most of the cattle have white faces, front of the neck, underbellies and tail tips and that good rich red on the rest of 'em. If the white strip of head hair doesn't stop midway above the shoulders, or if there's red hair mixed in with the white on the chest, or the white hair doesn't go all the way from the face to the end of the belly, that cow or calf is called a 'line back' and is culled.''

''You've used that term before. What does 'culled' mean?''

''It means cut from the herd, sold.''

''That seems rather…harsh.''

''Like I said, ranching is a business. These Herefords are the product of a long line of culling the undesirables. That and natural selection. These mountain strains have had to learn to adapt to heat and drought, cold and snow, and even the mountain lions and bobcats that range here, too. They're tough, they're strong, and I admire 'em. I admire the Parkers, too, for making this the ranch that it is. And the Hugheses. A Hughes has been here almost as long as the Parkers.''

"Christine told me your maternal grandfather owned a ranch in Central Texas," she said, hoping to draw him out more. "But he died when your mother and your aunt Delores were girls."

"That's right."

"So your mother came from a ranching family, too."

"Until she was twelve. Then my grandmother married a soldier stationed at Fort Hood and they lived lots of places after that."

"How did your aunt Delores meet your uncle, then?"

He smiled. "Uncle Dub managed to join the Army during World War II when he was only sixteen. He served for the last two years before the war ended…and no one ever caught on. He met Aunt Delores around then, married her and brought her back to the ranch. That's the only instance I know that he's been away from this place for more than a night, other than nine years ago when he had to go spend some time in the hospital. Broke his arm real bad when his horse fell with him. Happened not too far from here, actually. Took most of the next day to find him. No one was living out in Big Spur at the time."

"So that means you—" Katlin stopped. Maybe she shouldn't say it. It could reveal too much.

But he accepted that she'd done the math. "I've only been working for the Parkers three years this time," he said. "Don Simpson was here before me. And before him, for most of the years, there was no one steady. Regular ranch hands took turns patrolling the area off and on."

"Did they set up a camp because of your uncle's accident?"

"I'm not sure. Possibly. Whichever way, I'm glad they did."

"You truly like it here, don't you? You're not just saying it."

"I never 'just say' anything."

Because they'd reached camp—again, before Katlin knew where they were—she lost the chance to probe further. Quint took the horses off to care for them and she went to the motor home to try, once again, to relax. But she still couldn't. So much had happened this day. She would need time to sort through it all.

She was a little sore after six steady hours in the saddle, but a shower would take care of most of the light aches and pains.

There was a knock on her door. When she opened it, he smiled at her and her heart turned over.

"If you're hungry, there's plenty of beans and beef left over," he said.

"I—" She glanced behind her at the soup already heating on the stove.

"No problem," he said when he followed her gaze.

She waited for him to turn away. When he didn't, she adjusted her grip on the door. Tongue-tied, she could think of nothing to say.

He seemed to have the same difficulty. He looked from her, to his boots, then back up again. "I was wondering," he began.

"What?" she murmured.

"There's a place I know that might interest you. But when I go there, I usually stay overnight. Have to pack in, so it would be hard going."

"Harder than what we've already been doing?"

"A little. But it's worth it."

"What is this place?" she asked.

"It's a cabin I've been fixing up off and on over the past couple of years. An old trapper's cabin in a canyon with a small spring-fed creek. I'll sleep outside, so that won't be a problem. I just thought, since you liked what you saw today…"

"Is it in Big Spur?"

"Yes."

She shrugged, trying not to show her building excitement. He *was* starting to trust her! "Well, yeah, sure," she said. "That sounds great. When…do you want to go?"

"Tomorrow okay with you? So long as we leave by two we'll have plenty of time to get settled before dark." He narrowed his gaze. "Place is pretty spare. No electricity, no tap water, no fancy furniture."

She grinned. "You mean, like the fancy furniture I have here?"

He appreciated her humor. "You're living high here, lady," he teased. "In comparison."

A hissing sounded behind her—the tomato soup boiling over. She gave a cry of dismay and hurried to see to it.

"We'll talk more tomorrow morning," Quint called from the doorway. When she returned a moment later, he was gone.

Katlin shut the door and went back to clear up the mess. Soup was everywhere—on the stove, over the face of the counter, on the floor. She cleaned the stove and the counter, but when it came to the floor, after one swipe she settled in a soup-free area and rested her arms on her updrawn knees.

Was it a good idea for her to go with him to this cabin? Especially after what she'd thought earlier in the day? He obviously touched something in her emotions—whether she wanted him to or not.

She wasn't here to look for a boyfriend or a lover! She was here to find an answer for her parents. From the man who, as far as she could learn, was the sole person able to give her the information she needed. That she could entertain the slightest interest in him was a warped trick of fate.

Yet, she'd just come right out and told him that she liked him! Right after she'd put her foot in it and reminded him of her snooping.

At the time, she'd said it to allay his suspicion. But…she *did* like him!

She liked the way he was resourceful and intelligent, the way he looked at the land and his existence on it, the way he cared about all the living things populating the area, his quietness, his gentleness, his humor.

She'd been here less than a week! Last Saturday she'd been in Arlington, making last minute preparations for her trip. She'd decided to keep the apartment, at least until after she was finished in West Texas. Then she'd go back, pack her things and leave for California, where she would—where she would…*what?* She had no idea what she would do.

She wasn't the same person she used to be. Did she want the same things? Did she want to go back to the firm she'd once worked for and request another chance?

Katlin thought of the peace that had settled over her as she sat side-by-side with Quint on the plateau. A peace derived from the rugged timelessness of the land. A land unspoiled by the disruptions of modern life. And which conveyed to the individual who admired its stark beauty the idea that they, too, could survive.

QUINT WORKED WITH THE HORSES, brushing them, feeding them, checking their hooves and shoes.

When he was done, he stayed to watch them move around the corral.

What had started out to be a pretty awful day had turned brighter in the end—and he wasn't referring to the weather. His dark mood had lifted about the time he and Katlin had stopped on the rim.

He and Katlin.

Quint shook his head. This was starting to get a little…uncomfortable.

He wasn't sure why he'd asked her to the cabin. It had just popped out. Maybe it was the way she'd seemed so affected by the view at the rim—the way he could tell she was starting to feel about the land.

She was calmer about things now, from horses to snakes to…him.

She'd even told him she liked him.

Like. Just what a man wants to hear.

A woman likes a friend, likes a brother.

He didn't want that. He wanted more.

But just how much more, and for how long, he wasn't sure.

SUNRISE WAS BRIGHT AND BEAUTIFUL the next morning. Nature raised no objection to their plans.

As soon as Katlin saw Quint moving around she went outside to join him. She was a little self-conscious because of a dream she'd had. In it, Michael had told her that Quint McCabe was an ''okay guy''—his seal of approval for her boyfriends when she was growing up. Michael had then stepped out the door of her parents' house, dressed in his flight fatigues and looking just as he did in one of the photos she had of him. She'd pleaded with him to come back inside, so they could talk longer. She had questions she needed answered—about Quint. But Michael had grinned and winked and told her he had a mission.

Then she'd awakened and the moment dissolved. Michael's grin, his wink and his words were all she had left.

Quint's gaze flashed over her as she came to stand beside him, and she experienced an instant tug of attraction. To stop herself from doing anything about it, she slipped her fingers into her back pockets and rocked lightly on the soles of her boots.

"You look all energetic this morning," Quint said.

"Oh, I am," she agreed.

"Have you started putting your things together?"

"Yes. You said to bring enough for an extra day, right?"

He nodded. "You need to bring some bedding, too. A blanket—a couple if you have 'em. A pillow. A towel. Like I mentioned, the place isn't up to much."

"Do we need anything else?" She motioned to the small food sacks he'd assembled. "More food? More—" She ran out of possibilities.

"Got everything we need, I think. Flour, sugar, bacon, coffee. Pretty well keep to the basics."

"How do you cook?" she asked.

"On a campfire. There's no stove."

"It is primitive."

"Well, there's a stove, but I haven't got it working yet."

"Did you just happen onto the place?" she asked, curious.

"Nope. Most everybody on the ranch knows about it. It's just…remote."

"It sounds…interesting."

He responded to the ripple of trepidation he must have sensed in her voice. "If you don't want to go, we can call it off."

"Oh, no. No, really. I'd like to go."

"You're not exactly a rough-it kinda gal, are you?" he teased.

"Well, no…but I'm willing."

His eyes dropped to her mouth. He didn't say anything, but he didn't have to. He also didn't let his gaze linger, or let the moment drag on. Instead, he said, "When you finish getting your things together, bring 'em out."

"How are we going to carry everything?"

"On the horses."

"It won't be too much?"

He arched an eyebrow. "Just how much are you planning to bring?"

Katlin knew he wasn't serious, but she truly was

interested in how he planned to do everything. She decided to be patient, though. She would learn, eventually.

QUINT SPREAD a tarpaulin on the ground when he saw her step out of the motor home, carrying her things. Katlin had taken the time to fold the blankets, which he immediately shook open to place on the tarp, one atop the other. Then he took her clothes and laid them open down the middle, giving her pause when he deftly handled her more intimate items. Then he placed the bag with her toiletries near one end, and put her pillow near the other, before folding both sides of the blanket in and over to form a narrower line.

Straightening, he asked, "That's it, huh? No more?"

"That's it," she replied.

He moved to the end and started a roll from the bottom edge. Once he finished, the blankets formed an uneven cylinder, which he secured with a couple of strings.

"Later, we'll tie it behind the saddle," he said.

"You'll do the same to your things?" she asked.

"Yep."

"What about everything else—the food and the pots to cook in?"

"Food supplies go in the saddlebags. The cooking things are already there."

"Then…we're almost ready to leave?"

"Just about. We can start off any time we want. We don't have to wait until two."

Waiting was proving to be extremely difficult for Katlin. She needed to be active.

He must have read her thought, because he smiled with wry empathy, then said, "Meet you at the corral in a half hour."

Katlin was relieved. Only, she couldn't help but be reminded of the old saying—*out of the frying pan, into the fire*—which suddenly seemed a little too apropos.

THEY RODE OUT OF CAMP in yet another direction. Of necessity, Quint took the lead and Katlin fell into place behind him.

For a long time, their ride was little different than the ones they'd already made. Rough ground, patches of thick brush, areas where there was mostly grass, sharp inclines and descents. Then they started to climb in earnest. Mostly going up narrow trails. At times, they even had to dismount and walk ahead of the horses.

Katlin, panting after just such an exercise, was beginning to wonder if the change in place would be worth it.

The temperature was cooler and they might've been able to enjoy it, if they hadn't been working so hard to get where they were going. She saw no cows because, frankly, she didn't think the animals would be willing to climb to this point.

She was about to call for a halt when they rounded a curve at the edge of a cliff and came upon a beautiful box canyon glen where a one-room cabin, with weathered boards bleached almost the same color as the soil, sat not far from a narrow stream. The stream bubbled and gurgled gently from a point near the head of the canyon to where it disappeared down the far hillside past the trail. Several trees were scattered through the canyon, as was a certain amount of undergrowth. Yet in the center, along the stream and around the cabin, someone had cleared away the brush and high grass. The area was at the same time wild, yet tended. And altogether welcoming.

Katlin swept loose hairs away from her face after she dismounted. She was hot; she was tired. She wanted to be disgruntled. But she couldn't. Not here.

Quint had already swung down from the saddle and was busy removing his gear. She saw that he'd rolled his blankets and clothes in the tarpaulin, and carried his large thick-skinned bag and his rifle. At first, she was surprised that he'd included the weapon, but then, thinking about it, if a problem arose with a wild animal or anything else, she would rather he was able to deal with it.

She untied her bedroll and dropped it to the ground as he had. Then she removed the saddlebags he'd filled with the dry foodstuffs.

"What do you think?" he asked turning to her, his pale eyes intent.

"I think it's...absolutely lovely."

His unwavering gaze measured the depth of her feeling. What he saw must have satisfied him, because he relaxed and said easily, "Let me see to the horses, then we'll check the cabin."

He took the horses to a penned enclosure on the far side of the stream. A recent addition, the corral's wood rails had only just started to weather. "Boys are going to enjoy this," he said of the profusion of grass underfoot. He removed their saddles and bridles and slapped their haunches to signal freedom. "Yesterday's rain musta made it extra juicy."

"Do you think *they* think you come here just for them?" she asked as he rejoined her.

"Probably."

They gathered the gear they'd left on the ground and walked to the cabin.

"Don't forget. I warned you it was spartan," he cautioned.

"I won't forget," she promised.

He opened the door.

The interior of the cabin was as unprepossessing as the exterior. Besides the door, the one large room had a single window overlooking the stream, an old black pot-bellied stove with a broken vent pipe, and a simple wood-frame bed that sported a stretched canvas cover. On the stovetop sat a dented coffee pot, a Dutch oven and an old iron skillet. The shelf to one side held a trio of chipped plates and a large mixing bowl, while not far away a fuel-oil lantern hung from an exposed nailhead.

"You should've seen it before I started," Quint said. "There were holes in the walls, animals had made nests inside and a human of some sort had used the place as a garbage dump for a spell. It was pretty filthy."

She looked around. There were no more holes that she could see and the wood floor looked recently scrubbed. "And this was a trapper's shack?" she asked.

"A government trapper...years and years back."

"What did he trap?"

"Coyotes, for one thing."

"This far out?"

"A coyote never hunts near its den. They range pretty far."

"What else did he hunt?" she asked.

"Bobcats." He smiled. "So I wouldn't go wandering into any caves you might come upon. And there are mountain lions in the area, too."

She grimaced. "I think I'll stay close to you."

"Now that's an idea," he murmured. Then in almost the same breath he suggested, "Why don't you start making yourself at home? I have more things to see to outside. If you want something else to do, you can unpack the cooking supplies."

"Where do you want me to put them?" she asked.

"Shelf's fine. That's what it's for."

Katlin set about doing as he'd said. She refolded her clothes and stacked them on the foot of the bed once she'd spread out her blankets and fluffed up her pillow.

The conditions were indeed spartan. But she found them interesting. She could understand the challenge of seeing what you could do without.

She paused at the window on her way to the heaped saddlebags, curious as to what Quint was doing. She saw that he was with the horses, rubbing them down as they happily munched on the juicy grass. Then, as she watched, he reached for a large pail and poured it into a trough—water, from the stream. Then he went to get more.

She drew back from the window, reticent to have him see that she was watching. She'd observed him numerous times without him knowing it from the motor home, but the motor home's windows had coverings. Here, she was starkly in view.

She'd just finished putting the first batch of cooking supplies on the shelf when he walked back through the open door. For her comfort, she might have preferred that he knock or tap or give some kind of signal that he was entering, but Katlin rejected saying anything. He was, after all, sharing his secret place with her.

"You hungry?" he asked. "I've built a fire, so we should be in the food business pretty soon. And if you're thirsty—" his smile broadened "—come with me. I want to show you something."

She followed him out the door, then along the stream to the wall of the cliff.

"Look there," he said, pointing to where water burbled out of the rock partway up the sheer wall. Springing from numerous fissures, it collected in a naturally carved basin that fed the stream. "You don't get it much better than this," he said, and squatted down to rinse his hands in the stream before cupping them in the basin. Then straightening, he offered her his prize. "Have a taste," he said, grinning.

Katlin hesitated at the intimacy, then took a sip. "It's cold!" she exclaimed, drawing back, even as she wiped a dribble from her chin.

"You bet it's cold." He laughed and dropped the remaining water onto the ground. Then he dried his hands on his jeans and rubbed them together to warm them.

"But delicious!" she said, starting to enjoy the moment. "I'd like some more, please," she teased.

"You're going to have to get your next drink yourself," he said. "Either that, or find a cup."

"Oh, well, then—" Katlin murmured and bent down. But instead of dipping her hands fully in the water, she wet only her fingertips and straightening quickly, flicked the cold droplets on him. She laughed at his surprise, as freely as he had laughed at her. "You tricked me," she accused, backing toward the cabin, away from retribution. "You knew the water was cold when you offered it to me, but you didn't say a thing!''

He came after her at the same pace, smiling. ''I thought everybody knew a mountain spring would be cold.''

''I've never *seen* a mountain spring before.''

''Oh, well, then, that explains it. You've been deprived. Didn't know how to ride a horse, had never seen a rattler. Had you ever seen a live cow?''

''Of course I'd seen a live cow! Can I help it if these cows are different? And I *did* know how to ride a horse. I had lessons.''

''How many?''

''Three,'' she said.

''As many as that?'' Unexpectedly, he reached out and caught her, pulling her up against him.

Katlin hadn't meant for *that* to happen...or had she? She couldn't trust what she felt about him any more, or what she thought. Her mission seemed to be broadening, mixing, changing, softening. She'd once considered him to be her quarry...now she wasn't sure *what* he was.

She looked at him closely. The last time they were this near it had been at night, in a lantern's golden glow. Now she had the full impact of those blue eyes, as pale a blue as the sky. And his mouth, warm and exciting and—

''You don't want to get burned, do you?'' he questioned huskily.

Katlin couldn't drag her eyes away. She wanted him to kiss her!

"By the fire," he continued, and let go of her enough so that she could look around and see that he'd saved her from backing into the campfire.

A ring of stones surrounded a small bed of glowing coals not more than two steps from where they stood. Built permanently a short distance from the creek, Katlin hadn't noticed it when they'd come outside—but she remembered him having mentioned starting it.

She drew a soft breath. "I didn't know. I—" She felt the heat from the coals on the back of her legs, as well as the heat of embarrassment staining her cheeks. She made a move to twist away, but he stopped her.

"Not a problem," he said quietly. "You're safe."

And amazingly, for someone in such a precarious position, she believed him.

CHAPTER ELEVEN

KATLIN'S BODY TINGLED for a long time after he set her free. At first, she didn't know if she was relieved or disappointed. In her more lucid moments she knew it was better that nothing had started between them. But in her less lucid moments she wanted him to have kissed her until she lost all control.

The meal Quint prepared was pancakes and fried bacon, with honey as a sweetener. Katlin watched as he set the grill he'd pulled from behind the stove across the circled rocks, then adroitly worked the heavy iron skillet. Coffee was simply boiled spring water with a handful of coffee grounds added, then after the dented pot had been put aside to stew, a final splash of cold spring water—"to settle the grounds," he'd explained—just before service.

Katlin enjoyed the simplicity immensely. The coffee was strong, with a few errant grounds here and there, but it tasted full and rich—better than any she'd ever had in a coffee bar. The bacon had been fried crispy, just as she liked it. And the pancakes...she'd eaten three! Big ones.

"Oh, I can't move," she groaned.

He smiled as he ate his last bite of pancake. "Do

I remember something about you not eating much? Or is that an ungentlemanly thing to bring up?''

"I said it,'' she admitted. "I was wrong. Maybe it's the cook.''

"It's the fresh air and being busy. Always whips up an appetite.''

She considered him. "This wasn't spicy. Didn't you say you only knew how to make spicy things?''

He grinned. "I guess I forgot the jalapeño back at camp.''

"I'm glad you did. Hotcakes with jalapeño!'' She shuddered.

"I've had it before,'' he claimed. "Not bad, really. I'll make it for you when we get back.''

"I'll pass.''

"I thought you liked spicy food.''

"I do, but not for breakfast.''

"This isn't breakfast.''

"You know what I mean…breakfast foods.''

"What about *huevos rancheros?* You ever eat that?''

"No. I like my egg to be an egg. It can have cheese in it and maybe a little ham…but no onions or peppers or hot sauce.''

"What about grits?''

"Why do you care?'' she shot back.

His smile broadened. "You don't like 'em, do you? And you don't want to admit it.''

"I can eat them…sort of,'' she said defensively.

"California girl.''

"*Northern* California."

"I was in L.A. once," he said. "For a couple of days. Mostly a quick stop-over."

"What did you think of it?"

"It's big. Spread out like Houston is. Saw some oil wells, too. That surprised me. And some people were selling these huge strawberries on the side of the road."

"How long ago was that?" She felt a spurt of satisfaction that he was opening up, but at the same time, felt somewhat troubled about being pleased.

"Ten years, something like that. Maybe fifteen."

"What did you do there? Did you go to all the tourist spots?"

"A few. Not time to do much."

His legs were stretched out as he leaned back against the log he'd dragged forward for Katlin to use as a seat. All she had to do was reach out to touch his thick hair. Something she'd been wanting to do ever since they'd started eating.

"You never told me which part of northern California," he said, returning to the previous subject.

"A little place outside San Francisco."

"Does it have a name?"

"You wouldn't know it."

"Try me."

"Lafayette," she lied, naming a small town not far away from her even smaller hometown.

"That sounds like it should be in Louisiana."

"They're spelled the same, that's all."

"No alligators in your Lafayette, hmm?"

"No bayous, either." She switched topics this time. "You never said where you're from."

He was quiet a moment, then answered, "I'm from all over. My dad was career Army. I was born in Germany and raised...wherever he was posted. We moved around a lot."

She smiled. "So that's why you don't have a thick accent like most everyone else around here."

"Yep."

"Except the bits you've managed to pick up...like 'Yep.'"

He smiled lazily. "Kinda grows on ya," he drawled, in a good imitation of area natives.

"Yep," she returned, and they both laughed.

Quint started clearing away their clutter. He rubbed the iron skillet with a handful of sand, then rinsed it in the stream. Katlin did her part by copying his example with their dishes and forks.

"It'll get chilly later," he said. "I'll build us another fire. We have enough wood for that, but I'll need to get more for tomorrow."

Katlin followed his gaze to the small stack of wood he must have assembled on a previous visit. It wasn't the type of splits that her parents ordered from a service for their fireplace. This was broken branches and old fence posts.

"Would you like some help?" she offered.

"Nah." He reclaimed the rifle he'd left outside the cabin door. "There's a latrine over by those far trees, downslope from here. Not fancy, but it does the job.''

Katlin had started to wonder about that. ''Thanks,'' she said.

As she watched him go, moving easily as he carried the rifle balanced in one hand, she wondered if this was how women throughout the ages had felt as they watched the ''hunter'' leave camp. But then that would probably make her the hunter's ''mate''…which was beyond anything she wanted to deal with right then.

She turned away rather than let her eyes follow him and went to study the gurgling stream. She stayed at the water's edge for a time, then hopped over it to see the horses. Both came to greet her and she made fast friends with Jim, talking softly to him the way she did to Chili.

After that, she explored the area, finding the latrine he'd spoken of—little better than a shack, but at least it provided a modicum of hygiene and privacy—then she circled back to the cabin. Being here was like stepping back into the late nineteenth century. Probably even earlier, because the Indians who'd once inhabited this area of Texas must have known of the spring and visited it regularly.

She settled into the same place Quint had vacated earlier. Her back, like his, braced against the log. The sun had long ago moved behind the rim of the canyon, spreading the shadows of premature dusk.

She sighed and closed her eyes as, again, a sense of peace crept into her bones.

Her light doze was broken by a rustling not far away.

She remained as still as she could, while opening one eye. An antelope and two babies were drinking at the stream, close to the opening of the canyon.

Katlin held her breath. Because she'd been so still, the mother must not have realized she was there.

She watched as the mother lifted her head, sniffed…caught a fresh scent that caused concern and urged her babies away.

Only after they'd bounded off did Katlin sit up. The moment had been magical. Her parents had never taken the family on camp-outs. They'd done many things, but never that. She'd had no idea how wondrous such an experience could be.

Quint materialized, seemingly out of nowhere. He held a bunch of dried branches under one arm and the rifle, its barrel pointing toward the ground, resting in the crook of the other. "I don't suppose I need to ask if you saw them," he commented wryly.

"They were beautiful!" Katlin knew her face had to be shining with excitement. "I was dozing, then I heard them…and I watched as they got a drink. It was—" She suddenly was at a loss for words. "The babies were so sweet!"

"Lots of animals use this creek."

"Do you think we'll see more?"

"We might. But they'll mostly stay away until after we leave."

"Oh, I hope we see more."

He smiled.

"How often do you come here?" she asked, turning to watch him drop the freshly gathered wood next to the older stack.

"About every six weeks."

"How did you get to be so good at doing this kind of thing? I mean…if you moved around so much when you were a boy. Did your parents take you camping a lot?"

Quint laughed as he again stood the rifle against the side of the cabin. "No."

"Then how—"

"My dad lived and breathed the Army. He was a Supply Sergeant and never wanted to be anything else. When he wasn't working, he was thinking about working."

"And your mother?"

"My mother was a good Army wife. She kept the family going, just like my dad kept his Company going."

"So you didn't go on many vacations."

"We went places, but only when the government sent us. Lots of things to see and do when you live in a place for a few years."

"You don't have any regrets, then?"

She realized what she'd said the instant she said it. But the query had sprung from her own curiosity, not as part of any plan—her thoughts halted. For those moments she'd forgotten everything! What she was trying to accomplish here…why she *should* be peppering him with questions…questions, like the one she'd just asked, that would work to her advantage.

He shot her a look of slight irritation. "Of course I regret things. Who doesn't?" he demanded.

"I meant…about…growing up the way you did." She hoped she hadn't destroyed their burgeoning discussion.

Katlin could almost feel him stop himself from shutting her out.

He brought some of the larger pieces of wood over to the firepit and set them next to the stone circle. "I don't regret anything about the way I grew up," he said as he gathered what was left of the old coals and created a base for the new fire. "Do you?" he challenged.

"I—no, not really."

Katlin was growing weary of the continuing need to lie. She wanted to tell him the truth right then and get it over. He'd started to open up, to confide things she doubted that he'd ever told anyone. There was no longer a reason to delay.

But if she told him the truth about who she was, it would mean the end to everything. He'd either help her or not help her, and, either way, she'd have to leave.

Her reluctance to leave manifested itself as a

shooting pain through her midsection. She didn't want to go! Not yet. Not until after...*what?* After she decided whether she *was* starting to fall in love with him?

Or was that exercise coming a little too late?

After mumbling an excuse, she hurried into the cabin. She had to get away from him. She had to think. *Was* she falling in love with him? Had she *already* fallen in love with him? With the man who, at best, had been present when Michael died and, at worst, bore responsibility?

It couldn't be. It just couldn't be!

He tapped on the cabin door. "Are you all right in there? Are you sick?"

Katlin couldn't speak. Yesterday, she'd been presented with a possibility about what she felt for him...now, possibility was fast evolving into fact.

She cleared her throat, knowing she had to answer. "I—my stomach. I feel a little queasy."

In her mind's eye she could see his quick frown. His assumption would be that it was something she ate. The pancakes, the bacon. But since he'd eaten the same thing and wasn't unwell, the problem wasn't universal.

"Lie down for a while. See if that helps. If it doesn't—" He stopped. Their alternatives were limited.

"I—I'm sure I'll be fine," she answered, guilty at having created worry. "Just— Like you said, I'll lie down. I'm sure it's a temporary thing."

"Let me know if there's anything I can do."

"I will," she promised.

Oh, there was something he could do, but she didn't think it would make her feel better tomorrow. And it was tomorrow—all the tomorrows—she had to think about. She had to get herself under control. She *couldn't* let herself love him!

She settled onto the narrow bed. Not exactly the most comfortable place to wrestle with your psyche. Then again, maybe it was perfect.

QUINT WALKED SLOWLY away from the door, a deep frown creasing his brow. Had he just about killed her with his cooking, or what? She'd looked so stricken, then she'd run off.

He was angry with himself. Angry for being impatient with her. Angry for challenging her. Maybe she had things in her past, as he did, that were difficult for her to talk about. He knew so little about her!

Then again…he was coming to think he knew most everything he needed to know. He'd resisted having Mae Parker thrust her on him. Resisted having her ride along, asking questions. Now, he was starting to wonder—was it possible that he might not be meant to spend the rest of his life alone? And was she the person who might offer him a fresh start?

Love wasn't a word he tossed about lightly. He

knew its significance, had witnessed its power on
other men and, as a result, learned to be leery.

Still, when he glanced back at the closed
door...he found himself wanting to be with her.

TRUE DUSK HAD FALLEN by the time Katlin drew
herself into some kind of order and stepped back
outside.

Quint heard her coming and stood up. He'd been
sitting near the small campfire. "Are you better?"
he asked, concerned.

She nodded. She didn't trust herself to speak.
She'd known this first moment would be difficult.
Her gaze met his, then slid away. She couldn't pre-
tend, even to herself, to be wholly indifferent.

The branches sizzled and crackled as the low
flames transformed them into smoke and ash. The
air held a chill. Katlin stepped close to the fire and
extended her hands to the warmth. She'd donned her
jacket, just as he had.

"Think you can make the night?" he asked.

"I'm not ill," she said. "And even if I were, we
couldn't leave—ride in the night—could we?"

"That would depend on how bad things got."

He studied her intently, making her nervous. She
laughed, albeit unsteadily. "Well, you can call off
any emergency plans, because I'm all right. It was
just...indigestion. That happens sometimes. Doesn't
your stomach ever go funny?"

"Mine's made of cast iron."

"Then, just believe me. I'm okay."

He nodded, but he still motioned to the log. "Have a seat, why don't you? In a little while, when it gets completely dark, there's going to be a pretty nice show. The clouds have all cleared off and the haze is still thin. Gonna be lots of stars out tonight."

Katlin took her seat and looked up. The sky was changing from a rosy gray to a dark gray, even as she watched.

Quint came to sit where he had before, on the ground, next to her. After he stretched out his long legs, she sensed him exhale. Almost a sigh. She tried not to be so aware of him, but that was like asking a caged bird not to notice a prowling cat.

Minutes passed. Minutes in which neither of them said anything. The darkness deepened, surrounding them.

"Did you see it?" Quint asked, his voice sharp.

"What?"

"There was a shooting star…over there."

He pointed, but of course, the flash of light was over. She'd been looking but not seeing anything, her attention directed inward.

She slowly became aware of a canopy of stars emerging in the early night sky. Thousands of white twinkling dots.

"Just wait," Quint promised. "It gets better."

More time went by. Quint saw another shooting star, but again, Katlin missed it.

Finally, she saw one. "Oh! There! There, I saw that one. Did you?" she demanded excitedly.

"Sure did," he said.

She pulled her hand away from his shoulder the instant she became aware that she'd caught hold of it.

Katlin swiveled her head. Every direction she looked there were stars. Thousands and thousands of glowing stars. Big ones, little ones, dim ones, bright ones. Stars on stars on stars. The heavens didn't look big enough to hold them all. Their presence didn't seem real.

"It looks as if I can touch them, if I just...reach out—" She came to her feet and stretched out her hands, laughing in delight. "I've never seen so many in my life! They're wonderful, beautiful!"

A moment later she scooted back to her seat and turned to Quint. "Is this what it's like every night here? You get to see this? No wonder you like it so much. This is...spectacular!"

"Most nights it's spectacular," he confirmed, "but some nights, when conditions are right—like this one—it's extra special."

"I can't believe there are so many!"

"They're there all the time. Only most people don't take the opportunity to look at 'em. Being well away from a city helps, too."

"Oh, look! Another one!"

When she could finally pull her eyes away from the shooting star, she saw that he still watched her.

"Did you know it was going to be like this?" she asked.

He smiled slightly. "I had an idea."

"Because of the rain?"

He nodded.

Katlin knew she had to do something quickly. She could feel the tension building in him. Feel it building, unwillingly, in herself.

"You said—you said you worked on the Parker Ranch when you were a teenager, then you went away...and came back. What did you miss most when you were away?"

Questions again. She used questions like a shield.

The same thought must have occurred to him, but he didn't challenge her. He said quietly, "I can't really limit it to one thing. Mostly the silence, the way you're your own boss, the close balance with nature, the way one event follows another in the life cycle of the ranch. Just being a part of it all."

"What about this?" Her wave encompassed the starry sky.

He smiled. "No one place has an exclusive right to heaven."

"Did you miss going on roundups?"

"The later ones, yeah. Not the first couple. It takes a while before the other cowboys trust you when you're new. You get all the orneriest horses, all the worst jobs. You make mistakes that cause problems, like letting cattle spill when you're trailing 'em—some cows are always trying to break free.

Then you have to take a ragging from the men about what you did wrong. Most of the stubborn or skittish cattle hang to the back and that's where they put you. You spend your time swerving or slapping or yelling while trying to prod 'em on, and to make matters worse you're constantly fighting your horse. The dust is enough to choke you. Your body aches from the hard riding.''

''Why is it done that way? Why not encourage a new ranch hand? Why be so hard on him?''

''It's important to see what a person's made of. You need to see for yourself, too. Whether you can do it. After a time you get better, then you move up the social order.''

''Social order?''

''You're accepted because you know your job, because you can be relied on. Takes years to get really good at cowboying. Lots of experience.''

''What about when you left? Did you have to start over when you came back?''

Quint pushed another branch into the fire. Sparks danced in the rising smoke and burned out. ''Nah. It's like learning to ride a bicycle. You don't forget.''

''What—what did you do when you left here?'' She had a strong sense that this time he might tell her. She held her breath.

''I went into the Army, like my dad. Joined right after high school. It's what I'd been planning to do, and I did it.''

Katlin's heart skipped a beat. He'd mentioned his service in the Army himself. All along that had been the final point in her plan. Once he'd relaxed enough to admit his connection, she would know it was time.

The practiced words were on the tip of her tongue. *Were you there three years ago on December fifteen, when Michael Brown—my* brother, *Michael Brown—was killed in the line of duty? And if you were, what happened?*

She started to tremble, and he felt it, because he turned sharply to look at her.

"Katlin?" he murmured in a surprised, concerned way. Then he moved onto the log beside her, gripped her arms and tried to get her to look at him.

Katlin had had such trouble trying to control her emotions. Trying not to respond to him, when everything inside her urged her to. When, even at this definitive moment, she wanted him to fold her against him and hold on tightly. To keep her from saying what she'd planned.

"Katlin? What is it? What—?"

When he still didn't pull her against him, she leaned into him, turning her face into his shirt.

She felt him stiffen, even as his arms wrapped around her.

"What is it?" he demanded. "Are you ill again? Just how bad—"

The closeness of his body, his hard strength, his natural male scent engulfed Katlin's senses. She didn't want to think about what she should be doing or saying. God help her, she couldn't even think about Michael or their parents. Everything in her clamored for her to have what *she* wanted, without consideration of anything else.

As he spoke, as he questioned her about her wellness, she stirred, brushing her lips over the bronzed skin on his neck. His words stopped.

She felt his quick intake of breath.

Then as she continued to trail her lips over his skin, moving down to the open first button of his shirt, then back up to the underside of his chin, she could feel his heart hammer.

His embrace tightened, bringing her even closer, as his mouth hungrily covered hers.

Everything was forgotten as moment followed moment. Her fingers combed through his thick golden hair, reveling in the texture, in her license to at last touch it. Roamed over his shoulders, over his back, over his chest. She couldn't get enough of touching him...or of having him touch her.

Then something changed, and they drew apart, as if the intensity of their feelings had surprised them both.

CHAPTER TWELVE

KATLIN STARED AT HIM, just as he stared at her. They might have been at the threshold of a new world that neither was sure they wanted to enter.

Still…she wanted him to kiss her again. To more than kiss her.

He either sensed her need or listened to his own, because he leaned forward and touched his mouth softly to hers, moved to her ear, nuzzled it, then came back to her parted lips.

The kiss was long and heartbreakingly sweet, and despite knowing she shouldn't, she smiled tremulously at him when he straightened.

He smiled as well, only wryly. "Well, that kinda changes things, doesn't it?"

Katlin looked away, knowing it couldn't change *anything*.

He drew her chin back around. "And there I was, thinking something was wrong with you."

"I—I told you I was fine."

"Yeah, but—" He stopped. "Let's just say, I'll be glad to doctor you anytime. You're a heck of a lot more fun to take care of than a steer or a calf."

Katlin raised her hands to straighten her hair. As

short as it was, a shake of the head would have done, but she needed an excuse to break free. She also straightened her shirt, redoing a button that had come loose.

His gaze flicked over her, resting on the button. "Yep, a heck of a lot more fun."

"You know—you know this doesn't *mean* anything. Just because we— Because we— Don't read too much into it." Katlin knew she had to regain control. "You're a healthy male, I'm a healthy female. It's only natural. You, of all people, should understand that, what with your bulls and cows and stallions and mares."

"Oh, yeah," he murmured.

"I mean, you keep talking about them all the time. The way everything on the ranch is about procreation. Well, I'm not ready to procreate, and I don't think you are either. You said you weren't. And—and—"

Her strained little soliloquy drew to a stumbling close.

"Maybe we should call it a night, hmm?"

Katlin sprang to her feet, then she wondered about his use of "we." Wondered if he'd think she was anxious to jump into bed with him. Which she was, but not—

Oh, it was hopeless! She had to be by herself again to try to reorganize her thoughts. Try to forget once again what it felt like to be so intimate with him.

She glanced at him and saw that he was still smiling, as if her dance around the subject was amusing to him.

He stood up and swept her along as he walked toward the cabin.

Her heart rate increased. What had she done? She'd only made things worse. She couldn't sleep with him, then later tell him who she was.

He stopped at the door, then turned her to face him, his expression serious. "You're safe with me, Katlin. If you're not ready to take the next step, we don't take it. I'm not going to push. When you're gentling a colt you have to take it slow and easy, you have to convince him you're not the enemy. Same with a woman. I'm not your enemy. You don't have to be afraid I'll crash down your door. You don't need a lock to keep me out."

Katlin stared up at him. He didn't understand! It wasn't *him* she had to be afraid of. It was herself…and the feeling that seemed to be growing between them by leaps and bounds.

"Now, I'm going inside," he explained, "but it's to find your lamp so I can get it going for you. And if you'd like company back and forth to the latrine, just say the word. Stay here a second."

He disappeared into the darkness and came out again, carrying the lantern. He took it into the light of the campfire, made a few motions, then walked back with it emitting a soft glow.

"I'll put it on the stove for now, okay?" he asked.

She nodded.

At the stove, he said, "Don't be worried about it exploding or anything. It's perfectly safe to use. You can take it with you wherever you want to go. When you want it off, just press the little lever on the side, the glass'll lift, and you blow out the flame. Easy as pie."

Katlin nodded again. He was being so nice, trying to see to her every need, because he knew she was a novice at camping. "Thank you," she murmured.

He returned to the door, and as he drew abreast, Katlin was reminded of the first time she'd seen him, the day she and Morgan Hughes had arrived at Big Spur. He'd looked the epitome of a working cowboy, holding a saddle in one hand and a bridle in the other. He hadn't seemed real to her then. Now he felt too real.

Her gaze moved over his handsome features, careful to avoid his eyes but dwelling for a second on his lips. Then she took a tiny step back, easing his passage outside.

He gave a little nod and walked on.

THE NIGHT SEEMED TO LAST forever. Katlin heard many of the same sounds as she had her first night in Big Spur. Only she was closer to more of the sources here than she ever had been in camp. The sounds weren't what kept her awake, though. Scruples did.

She got up a number of times, almost always to

look out the single window. And each time, Quint was in the same spot—in a bedroll, close to the flickering embers of the campfire, which eventually turned cold over the hours of her intermittent watch. He was keeping his word.

He seemed completely at ease sleeping rough, as seen by the stars and the moon that had finally put in an appearance to bathe the glen with its light. He didn't toss and turn as she did. He didn't pace.

All she could think about was the situation.

Why him? Why her? Why now?

And what was she going to do about it?

SOMEONE NUDGED her arm. She moaned as she rolled away. She would swear that she'd just closed her eyes.

Her eyes popped open as she remembered where she was, what had happened and who the "someone" had to be.

She held the blanket close to her chin as she struggled to sit upright. The bed didn't make that kind of movement easy.

"Morning." He smiled down at her. "Thought I was going to have to play Prince Charming for a second there." He offered her a cup of coffee. "Thought you might like some of this before it gets strong enough to walk away. Biscuits are almost done, too."

"B-biscuits?" Katlin was having a hard time dealing with the fuzz left in her brain by sleep and by Quint's notion of playing Prince Charming as he stood next to her bed.

"Luckily the eggs I packed didn't break, so we'll be having them, too. Sound good?"

"I—yes."

His smile was freer than she'd ever seen it. "About ten minutes, then," he said and left the cabin.

Katlin wanted to slide back down between the blankets. To pull the top cover over her head in order to shield herself from reality. But she couldn't do it. Not with a cup of coffee in her hand. And by the time she'd maneuvered to where she could set it on the floor without spilling it, she might as well have gotten up.

She swung her jeans-clad legs out of bed and stood in her stocking feet. She hadn't trusted herself enough last night to change into her gown. She ran a hand through her hair after pulling her boots back on, took a sip of the strong brew, then stepped shufflingly outside.

The morning was still slightly cool, but the sun had long broken the horizon. The campfire coals were already glowing—the Dutch oven set to one side of the grill, the coffeepot closer to the center. Wonderful aromas teased her appetite.

"Ah…is there any chance of getting some warm water to wash with?" she asked Quint, who was just returning from the spring basin, carrying a full pail.

"Sure thing," he said.

He filled their only bowl partway from the pail, then added clear water from the coffeepot.

"Should be about right," he said.

Katlin tested it. "Perfect," she agreed. "Thanks."

"Don't mention it."

Katlin didn't see how the two of them being thrown together so closely could continue. Not when she had her secret.

She retreated into the cabin, fortified herself with another swallow of coffee, did her best with the wash water and dressed in fresh clothes. Then, after a quick trip to the latrine, she finished getting ready, combing her hair and adding a little lipstick. The lipstick served as a reminder of who she was. That she had another life. A life that needed resolution, before she could—

Before she could, what? Reclaim her own life? Reclaim it with Quint? Or at least, see if what she had started to feel for him was real? Not to mention what he felt. Because once she told him who she was, how was *he* going to react? Her entire presence here was a lie. Even down to her last name.

She groaned quietly to herself. She'd spent most of last night thinking about this, and had yet to reach a comfortable conclusion.

When she went back outside, his eyes moved over her, noting the change of clothes, probably noting the lipstick, too. As he started frying bacon, she went to stand at the stream to look around.

The cold, clean water gurgled and bubbled as it moved over the rocky ground. Chili and Jim seemed content in their corral. Insects and birds went about their daily game of hide-and-seek. All was as it should be in the world. Except her world.

Katlin sighed restlessly and went to wait beside him.

"Is there anything I can do?" she asked. "I'm starting to feel useless."

He looked up from where he was crouched. "All that's left is the eggs. And I'm planning to fry them after this. You can get the plates, if you want."

Happy for something to do, Katlin returned to the cabin. She gathered the plates and forks...then for the first time realized that he must have crept into the cabin earlier in the morning in order to have so much of the breakfast already prepared. All the ingredients, plus the limited cookware, were kept inside. She'd seen them last night, stacked in place on the stove and the shelf, when she'd blown out the lantern.

It gave her a funny feeling when she thought about him seeing her asleep. In all likelihood, he'd come in and out more than once. But at no time had he transgressed. Had he paused to watch her, though, as she'd watched him last night in the moonlight?

She shivered at the intimate thought, then tried to tell herself it was the morning chill. But she knew it wasn't.

AFTER BREAKFAST, Katlin still couldn't settle. Just as she couldn't sit on the log to eat, or have him come too near. His spirits seemed to be rising, though, as the morning progressed.

She washed up—at her insistence—while he went to see to the horses. He spent quite a long time with them, giving them some oats that he'd brought along, checking their legs and shoes, patting them, talking to them.

Then, whistling, he stepped back across the stream. He came to where she stood, her hands in her back pockets, moving bits of dirt with the toe of her boot.

"You about ready to head back?" he asked.

"Head back?" she echoed.

"Did you think I was going to hold you captive here forever?"

"I like it here."

"Sure, I do, too," he agreed. Then, eyes narrowing, he asked carefully, "Are you telling me you want to stay?"

"No!" she answered quickly, in too much of a hurry to frame a better reply. "I mean...it's—it's beautiful here, but...I'd like to get away from it in order to write up my notes. I—I never can do that on the spot. I have to be away."

More lies. Katlin knew she should be made to bite her tongue severely as punishment. But she had a terrible feeling that later, she would consider such a penalty light.

"Maybe one day we can come back."

Quint's suggestion held multiple layers of inference. Katlin chose to stay close to the surface. "Sure," she said airily. "We might have time again before I have to leave."

His eyelids flickered, but he didn't press the subject further.

They packed up, returning the glen to the condition they'd found it. Quint readied the horses, then they mounted and rode away.

Katlin couldn't resist a long look back just before they rounded the side of the cliff. It was such a beautiful spot. A jewel hidden in the harsh landscape. She strove to imprint it in her mind.

Would she ever see it again?

Chances were...not.

THEIR JOURNEY AWAY from the cabin proved slower than their journey there. Most of the time they were going downhill and frequently had to get out of the saddle to lead the horses.

At such times Quint maintained a close watch on her, even reaching out to assist her in places where she might stumble.

Once they arrived at comparatively less difficult ground, he was still attentive. He started to point out things, telling her the names of various vegetation. The thorny mesquite and creosote bushes, the multi-armed ocotillo cactus, the sharp leaves of the yucca—Spanish dagger, he said it was also termed.

He pointed out a roadrunner, a red-tail hawk, a quail and various lizards. He was the complete opposite of the taciturn man he'd once been.

Conversely, Katlin wanted him to stop talking. Her nerves were frayed from too little sleep and too much worry. She longed for the solitude of her motor home. She *had* to work out what she was going to do.

Quint pulled up to ride beside her when the brush thinned. His night's growth of beard was a darker, reddish color in the full sunlight. The effect, with his pale eyes and bronze skin, was exhilarating.

She'd been kissing him last night for all that she was worth and he'd returned the compliment. It could happen again—right then!—if she wanted. All she had to do was ask.

She rolled her shoulders and shifted her position in the saddle.

"Won't be long," he said encouragingly.

She nodded and felt his gaze linger.

"You're very quiet," he said.

"I'm tired."

"Is that all?"

"Isn't that enough?"

"Depends what you're tired of."

"I—I didn't sleep very well last night."

"Problems with the bed?" he asked smoothly.

"That and...other things." She sent him an irritable look. "You didn't have any trouble sleeping, though, did you?"

"How do you know that?" he asked, his slow smile growing.

"I looked outside. You never moved."

"Did you come outside?"

"No!"

"Did you *want* to come outside?"

"I—"

He nodded. Her pause had given him the answer.

They rode in silence. Then, almost as if he'd been searching for a safe subject, he offered, "I can tell you something about cows and calves you might not know."

"That's a pretty safe bet," she returned drolly.

"Did you know that when it comes to a cow recognizing her calf, the legal authorities in cattle country will take her word over anyone's? She's so good that when we separate the pairs at spring roundup to work the calves, and later put 'em all back together in the same pasture, each cow, without fail, will find her own calf. Even when there's four or five hundred babies to choose from, all looking exactly alike, momma's never wrong. They do it by scent. That's gotten more than one rustler in trouble over time."

She glanced at him.

"That's what Morgan used to do—" he continued "—go after rustlers for a big ranchers' organization. Liked to call himself a cow cop. He was thinking about applying for the job the first time I came to live on the ranch. According to him, rustling's as big a problem now as it was in the old days. The thieves just use different methods. Back up big trucks to a cut they make in the fence and herd 'em in.''

''Is that why you have to be so careful about keeping watch on the fences?''

The fact that she'd finally asked a question seemed to please him. ''There aren't any roads coming into Big Spur except the private one, and we're surrounded by other divisions or mountains like what we've just been in. No big-time rustler would bother with Big Spur. They like things to be nice and easy, otherwise they'd raise cattle themselves. Small-timers, now that's a different story. They use pickup trucks or horse trailers and pick you off a few at a time. Still not much of a problem in Big Spur, but some of the other divisions have had trouble on occasion. They can get in and out before you even know they've been there. It's particularly bad if a calf hasn't been branded yet and the rustler, caught near red-handed, denies what he's done.''

''Which is another reason why it's important that a cow knows her calf, and that the authorities believe her,'' she deduced.

''You got it.''

Katlin smiled in spite of herself. She liked the way he'd worked the story. She still had her same question, though. ''Then if Big Spur isn't at risk from rustlers, why do you keep such close watch on the fences?''

"To keep the cattle in the right pastures. In some we have pairs, in others we have steers and replacement heifers it's too early to breed. We don't want 'em in with the bulls yet."

"What would happen if a heifer got pregnant too soon?"

"Usually, she's never a good producer and you end up having to cull her."

Katlin knew better than to voice any censure. That was the way things worked on this ranch, and had worked for generations. She settled for, "I think I prefer to have pets."

"Do you have any?" he asked curiously.

"Not now. I used to."

"Why not now, if you like them so much?"

She answered without thinking. "I'm never home."

He frowned. "So you go out on a lot of research trips?"

"For—for articles, yes," she lied again.

The camp came into view and Katlin felt a surge of relief, because every time she answered with a falsehood, she added to the complication.

He would remember each and every instance.

With little more than a mumbled, "See you later," Katlin escaped into her motor home.

Though her use of the recreational vehicle had been short, its familiarity was reassuring. She could be herself there…whoever *that* was. She could also tell herself she *had* to do what she'd come to do...even if she was starting to find it more and more difficult.

She took a shower and found it wonderful to be really clean, but the shower could do nothing to solve her problem. And it was barely one o'clock! An entire day could have passed, considering the way she felt.

She looked out a side window, curious what Quint was doing. When she saw him striding toward her door she hurried to open it. She was determined that when they met again it would be on her terms.

The soft chink of spurs told her what he planned to do even before he spoke. He hadn't worn spurs to the cabin, because he hadn't intended to work cattle.

"Are you going out again so soon?" she asked.

"Yeah, I saw some fence on the way in that needs a second look." His eyes moved over her appreciatively. "You sure smell good."

"It's soap. I wouldn't have minded if you'd stopped earlier."

"Didn't have the right tools with me. Can't do much with a sack of flour and a handful of coffee beans."

His little jest drew a smile from her.

"Now that's what I like to see," he said approvingly.

"What?" Katlin asked, but she knew. Her smile disappeared.

"Damn," he murmured.

His pale eyes never once left her face.

Katlin shuffled her bare feet, then the next thing she knew he wrapped an arm around her waist and pulled her out of the motor home. As had happened before when he'd carried her on Jim, her feet dangled in the air. Only this time, when he held her, most of her body was against his.

"I just want to see something," he explained, and his lips found hers.

Again, the kiss was long and wonderful and brought every inch of Katlin to intense life. Then it was over. He set her back on her feet in the doorway and grinned. "Just making sure I hadn't been dreaming," he said, after which he touched the brim of his hat and turned to walk away.

Katlin didn't know whether to sputter or swoon. *Damn* was right!

He stopped. "I almost forgot. I came to tell you that if you need it, there's a washer and dryer in the kitchen. They're both small, but they do the job. Feel free to use 'em. I'll probably be out for two or three hours. Got a couple of other things to check while I'm at it."

The good manners Katlin's mother had insisted upon rose unconsciously to her lips. "Thanks. I appreciate it."

He touched his brim again and winked.

Katlin quickly closed herself back inside. Oh,

yeah…a lot of good being determined to meet him on her ground had done her. He'd just swept her off it!

KATLIN VENTURED OUT after she saw Quint ride away. She wished she didn't have to take him up on his offer of a washer and dryer, but if she didn't, she would have to wash some things in her tiny kitchen sink. Either that, or wear them the next time she was in the shower. Neither option appealed. Her week's worth of jeans was exhausted, except for the pair she now wore. And her supply of everything else was getting low. The prospect of having several changes all clean and dry in less than a couple of hours brought her to his trailer.

As before, the door was unlocked. As before, she went inside. But this time she looked at it with different eyes. She no longer checked for evidence of his past life. He'd told her more about himself outside the Army than she'd ever expected. This time she was seeing it as an extension of the man she'd come to know.

Again, she noticed how much he seemed to appreciate order. Few things were out of place. All his military training, she reckoned. Michael had been the same way when he'd come home on leave. He'd made his bed as soon as he got out of it, put his clothes away, kept any surfaces cleared and his closet organized.

Katlin didn't search in any of Quint's drawers or closets on this visit. She went straight through the

living room into the kitchen and opened the narrow
pantry doors on the far side of the stove. She had a
vague memory of seeing a washer and dryer there
on her last trip into the trailer. Their presence hadn't
interested her then. Now, she found an over/under
space-saving type that she'd never used before.

She loaded her soiled clothing, added some of the
washing powder from a nearby shelf and started the
machine. Then she headed back outside. But a crumpled sheet of paper on the floor in the living room,
between a trash basket and a worn recliner, caught
her eye. She stopped, battled her conscience, then
left the paper where it was.

The wash required further attention, though. She
had to return to make the switch. And this time, she
couldn't resist.

She smoothed open the plain white sheet and read
the single line jotted below the date: *Mom, I think
I'm finally starting to understand why you followed
Dad around the world for all those….*

A strong masculine script, incomplete. A snippet
of thought, put to paper today, shortly after they'd
come back from the cabin.

Breathing shallowly from her latest duplicity,
Katlin recrumpled the paper and returned it to its
original position. He hadn't meant for anyone but
his mother to read it. And then, possibly not even
her. The woman wouldn't receive the note unless he
rewrote it.

Katlin wished she hadn't noticed. Wished she

hadn't snooped. Wished her thoughts hadn't immediately jumped to their own conclusion.

If she reasoned correctly and those few words were an insight into what he thought, he was grappling with the same possibilities as she was. Which meant that what was happening between them truly counted for something. For both of them.

Not that it was fully formed. But, again, the possibility was there. A possibility that was getting stronger for him as well. Strong enough for him to confide on paper. Strong enough for her to—

She bit her bottom lip and hurried out of the trailer.

She had to tell him. And tell him soon. Before either of them could be hurt too badly.

CHAPTER THIRTEEN

THE TIME BEFORE Quint's return was torturous. Katlin folded her clothes and put them away, then stretched out on her bed with a photo of her family hugged close to her breast.

The snapshot had been taken the last summer Michael was home on leave. They'd all gone to the beach on an unusually warm day for the northern California coast. Jackets had been left in the car as they walked on the sand. A friend had taken the picture and managed to capture the joy they'd felt at being together again. Michael had his arms across both his ''girls''' shoulders, while their father held up a seashell to examine. All were smiling, carefree.

Katlin studied their faces. Her parents looked much younger than they presently did, emotional pain having aged them far more than the nearly five calendar years since the photo was taken. She herself looked innocent and unsuspecting, her world seemingly assured. And Michael—who'd been thirty-five when he died—would forever be thirty-three, as he was here.

She smoothed a finger across his cherished features and wished she had him to talk to. But if she did, she wouldn't be here, faced with this terrible quandary.

The muffled sound of a horse's hooves caused her to sit up. Quint had returned to camp.

Minutes ticked by as she waited for him to do whatever it was he usually did after coming back from riding pasture.

She would tell him the truth, the full truth…about everything. Now.

HE SMILED when he stepped out of the tack room and saw her. His wonderful, easy, sexy smile that made her knees weak each time he used it. His expression was warm with pleasure, as if he thought she'd come expressly to greet him.

"I like having you here to say hello," he said, as he slipped an arm around her waist.

It felt so right to have him hold her that way. To have him smile down at her. To give her a soft kiss.

"I'm pretty rank," he said, straightening. "I could sure use a shower. How about, when I'm done, we think about eating dinner? I've got a sauce that tastes pretty good on spaghetti. We can cook some up and pour it on—"

"I— Quint—"

"You know? I think that's the first time you said my name and didn't say it like it hurt."

"Quint—"

He started to bring her along with him to his

trailer, but Katlin held back. Her resistance made his smile disappear. "What's up?" he asked.

Even with the ample opportunity she'd had to prepare, Katlin didn't know how to begin. "I—I think I should leave Big Spur," she said starkly.

Her announcement took him by surprise. "Why?" he demanded.

"It would probably be for the best."

"Why?" he repeated.

"There's something I have to explain."

He looked at her for a long time, before saying levelly, "Can I get my shower first?"

She nodded, even though she'd rather that he didn't. She wanted to get the whole thing over and done with and, hopefully, settled to where he'd understand.

"I'll meet you back here in ten minutes," he said. Then he went inside.

THOSE WERE THE LONGEST ten minutes in Katlin's life. They felt even longer than the hour she'd spent, waiting for him to return to camp. She paced the yard. The motor home was too small to be in right now. She'd go crazy inside—feel constrained, trapped.

Trapped in a web of her own making.

But she'd had no alternative! The only way to proceed had been the way she'd done it. None of the people she'd talked to about Michael's "accident" in the two years it had taken her to ferret out

Quint's name had wanted to talk to her initially.
She'd had to shame them into it, bully them. And
she'd known that Quint, more than any other, would
resist talking to her. He'd hidden himself away on
the ranch so successfully that extreme measures had
been needed just to see him.

The last thing she'd expected was to be attracted
to him, or even more shatteringly, to find herself
starting to fall in love.

Time was compressed in this place. The act of
discovery accelerated. She'd learned things about
Quint in a short few days that could take years to
emerge in normal life. She'd witnessed his strength,
his humor, his caring nature…and to add to that, his
almost irresistible physical appeal.

Katlin continued to pace. She couldn't stay still.

QUINT HELD IT TOGETHER while he took his shower.
He didn't want to jump to conclusions. Just because
Katlin had said she wanted to leave didn't mean she
actually did…or would. Women were one of life's
greater mysteries, and he doubted he'd ever truly
understand. His sister had married a man he didn't
think much of, but she swore she loved him. Now
nearly twenty years and three children later, they
were still together and seemingly happy. His mother
had followed his father all over the world for as long
as his father lived, knowing that she came second to
his career. She'd loved him and he'd loved her, but
the Army had always come first.

Which was a good part of the reason Quint had never married. He wouldn't put a woman through that. As long as he'd been in the Army, he'd never looked for anything permanent. Then he'd gone through the trouble in Manzant and made his decision to protect the Colonel. Dishonor wasn't something he wanted to visit on a woman either. But Katlin had made him start to wonder.

He hadn't gotten around to actually thinking he'd tell her his story. He wasn't sure enough about anything—about her—to share something so private. And there were parts he couldn't *ever* tell her—couldn't tell anyone—because of the confidentiality clause in the separation agreement he'd signed when he resigned his commission. Not to mention the high-level classification the government had placed on anything concerned with the mission.

He pulled on fresh clothes and swiped a comb through his hair. He needed a shave, but he'd do that tomorrow. At least it would be something to look forward to, since all else was up in the air.

Katlin sat perched on the edge of a chair under the awning. She jumped when he opened the door. Worry clouded her expression.

He wanted to bring her into his arms and offer what comfort he could for whatever had upset her, but he stepped to the remaining chair instead.

"Okay," he said, sitting down. "What's this you have to explain?"

She gave an almost imperceptible twitch. "I—

well, first—my name isn't Katlin Carter...and I'm not a writer for *Eyes On Texas* magazine. I'm not a writer at all.''

His body stilled as his thoughts leaped to his last mission. Shortly before his formal resignation, there had been a couple of members of the local press sniffing around the base, acting as if they knew something. Quint had talked to neither. Nor, apparently, had anyone else. And their interest had died. Was Katlin a hired investigator or some kind of news producer, bent on resurrecting the story? He quickly ran through all the things he'd told her about himself, particularly his time in the Army. He could remember saying nothing more than that he'd been in the service.

''What are you then, if you're not a writer?'' he asked flatly.

''I'm just...a person.''

He remained silent. She was nervous enough and unsettled enough that she would soon say more.

She swallowed tightly. ''I—does the name 'Brown' mean anything to you?''

''Should it?'' he returned with clipped brevity.

''How about a little over three years ago...a week-and-a-half before Christmas? Sergeant Michael Brown.''

Sergeant Michael Brown...the helicopter crew chief who'd died, along with the two special forces guards. Their names, as well as what he remembered of their faces, had been seared into his mind.

She continued, "I'm Katlin Brown...Michael Brown's sister."

Quint felt as if he'd been hit with a poleax. Sweat broke over his body. Breath seemed nonexistent. Katlin was— Katlin claimed to be—

He was thrown back into the chaos of those moments when he, the guards and the suited man were running for the helicopter...when they were trying to get the injured on board...when the crew chief was hit in the forehead as he tried to help...then the pandemonium that had erupted as they lifted off and attempted to save the flickering lives, to no avail.

He stood up to complete several steps, before pivoting to face her. "Your brother?" he said hoarsely.

"My older brother. He—he died." Emotion temporarily overwhelmed her.

KATLIN KNEW she didn't need to tell him that last part. He already knew. But the words seemed necessary.

Her eyes moved over his lithe form, hunched slightly as if wounded. His expression, though controlled, was stricken.

Was it guilt that made him react so palpably? Guilt over Michael's death?

She twisted her fingers, rubbed her palms.

"What do you want?" he demanded. "Why are you here?"

"I need to ask a few questions. About Michael. About what—"

"I can't tell you anything."

"Can't...or won't? Quint, I really need you to answer my questions."

He continued to look stunned, continued to seem to have difficulty following what she said.

She wanted to reach out to him, to tell him that whatever had happened, they could deal with it. If she was willing to accept that Michael might have made a mistake that led to his death and the death of two others, she could do the same for Quint. In the beginning she might not have been able to, but that was before she'd gotten to know him. He and Michael held to the same ideals. It would be much the same situation for both of them—a good man, caught in the middle of something terrible, making a mistake.

"I *can't!*" he said in answer to her previous challenge. He turned away again, moved a few additional steps, then realized what she'd admitted to earlier. "You lied," he accused her, swinging around. "Everything you said...all those days! You lied to the Parkers. You lied to me."

"For good reason! Quint, please listen!"

He avoided her touch when she reached for his arm. "You brought me along, got me to where I—" His laugh was ironic. "You must have found it all pretty funny!"

"That's not true!" she denied. "I never thought it was funny. Not any of it! I'm here for a reason. I have to know what Michael did that day—that night—I don't even know when it happened, except it was December fifteenth!'' She jumped up, caught hold of his arm and wouldn't let go. ''I'm not here to make trouble for you, Quint. Not for you or for anyone. I don't care about any of that. I just have to know...did Michael cause the accident? Did something he did or didn't do cause those soldiers to die...cause him to die?''

''What?''

She hurried on. ''I've spent almost three years trying to find an answer. Locating people Michael knew. His friends, his crews. Finally, someone told me *you* were the person I needed to talk to. That you were there. You would know. I traced you as far as the ranch. Then I had to come up with a way to get inside. I couldn't just drive to Big Spur. The Parkers have a reputation...you know their reputation. You uphold it. What would you do to a stranger who just showed up? So, I *had* to lie. To Mae Parker, to you. I knew you'd never agree to talk to me otherwise. Look at you now!''

He didn't relent. ''I don't appreciate being lied to. Not after—''

Katlin knew what he meant—after things had changed between them.

''I was afraid to tell you! Again, look at you now. You aren't even trying to listen to what I'm saying! I'm trying to explain, yet you—''

''You sure had me fooled. I was beginning to think—''

"I know! But I didn't fool you in that way, Quint. What happened between us…it took me as much by surprise as it took you. I wasn't looking for someone to—to care about, and neither were you. It just…happened."

"You still should have told me."

"I'm telling you now."

"Well, maybe that's not good enough."

Katlin grew desperate. "Quint, *please,* was Michael responsible for what happened? My mother and father—the officer who came to see them left them with the idea that they should stop making inquiries because they might not like what they discovered. That Michael might be to blame for everything. But it wasn't my parents making the inquiries…it was me! *I* was the one asking for answers. I just made the mistake of asking the wrong people. I thought the Army *owed* us a better explanation."

"What were you told?" Quint demanded tightly.

"Very little. Just that Michael died on December fifteenth in an accident, out of the country and that two others died at the same time. It—it's torn my parents' lives apart. The officer made it sound so—so awful that they're afraid to ask, and because they're afraid, they're in limbo. They can't move on. And they both— I can't stand to see what's happened to them! What the officer did made me angry, and I kept asking questions, only I stopped using formal channels. I went to anyone who might know anything."

While she spoke Katlin was aware that Quint had been closing more and more into himself, even as anger sparked off him.

"The officer was mistaken," he said roughly. "What happened *wasn't* your brother's fault."

Relief washed over Katlin. Her long-term crusade had at last brought its reward. She could tell her parents with assurance that Michael wasn't to blame, free them of the poisonous venom that had made them so vulnerable.

Her eyes fluttered open and she gazed at Quint. There was more. "What did happen?" she asked quietly. "I know you left the service shortly after the—"

The look in his eyes held her to the spot, prevented her from completing the sentence.

"That's all I'm going to say," he returned, tight-lipped as he pointedly removed her clinging fingers from his arm. "The officer got it *wrong*."

"Quint, I need to know you understand I didn't do this purposefully!" She meant fall in love with him, or try to get him to fall in love with her.

"We've said it all, haven't we?"

"No! I—"

He brushed past her, heading for the door.

"Quint!" she cried, unable to hold back any longer. "I think I love you!"

He stopped and turned, his expression set. "What am I supposed to do about that now?" he demanded harshly. "Believe you? When you've already shown you're willing to say or do anything to get what you want?''

"I did it for my parents, Quint. For Michael!"

He didn't reply, merely looked at her with icy renunciation before disappearing inside the trailer.

QUINT COULD BARELY contain himself. He felt under assault from all sides. She'd lied to him! What had happened between them this past week had been based on nothing. He couldn't even be sure she was who she claimed to be right this very minute! She wouldn't be the first person to assume another identity the instant the first was found out.

Yet if she was telling the truth, at least as far as what her family had been told about Sergeant Brown's death, the Army brass had lied as well. *He* had taken the blame for what had happened in Manzant. He'd given up his years of service, allowed his name to be discredited, borne the shame...and someone—possibly someone under orders to keep a lid on—had gone to Sergeant Brown's home and left his parents—her parents?—with the impression that their son was responsible. How far up the chain of command had that directive originated? And if it was a concerted effort and not one officer going off on his own, then it meant that he, Quint, had made the sacrifice for nothing!

Quint paced the floor.

He could do little about it, though, other than what he just had. But what about the other men who had died that night? What had their families been told? They were special forces, though, and their notifications might have been handled differently. As well, their families might have been more aware of risks and procedures.

He thought about what Katlin had said of her parents—her purported concern for them being the reason for her deception. His anger continued to roil. The brass had been quick to slap the highest classification on the operation, probably at the direction of those civilian entities involved with the suited man. They wanted everyone to forget that night in Manzant.

He'd left the military under a cloud; the other soldiers had been buried. Including Colonel Tucker, who'd died just six months after suffering his stroke.

If he said anything to anyone now, it would only serve to stir up trouble posthumously for the Colonel and for Agnes, who continued to enjoy the benefits accrued through the Colonel's lifetime of exemplary service, and who still could hold proudly to her husband's good name.

Quint slumped into the recliner and stared into empty space. He did his best not to think about anything.

KATLIN THREW HERSELF on her bed in the motor home. She'd expected him to react badly, but this was worse! He'd rejected her wholly and completely, and nothing she said or did could make a difference. Not even when she told him she thought she loved him.

He'd been almost beside himself with anger—directed at her and at what her parents had been told by the officer. But mostly at her.

It had cut deeply when he'd said that about her being willing to say or do anything to get what she wanted…but unadulterated truth *did* cut deeply. She had been willing to do either. To anyone. She had placed gaining the truth about Michael above everything else. Placed her parents' anguish above any anguish she might inflict. Had she really given much thought to the consequences Tessa Goodall might face if Malcolm Thompson ever found out that she'd let Katlin use his signature pen on her letter to Mae Parker? Or that Tessa had vouched for her to Mae Parker when she called, confirming that "Katlin Carter" planned to write a series of articles for the magazine? Had she concerned herself with any of the people in active military service she'd questioned, who might have put their careers at risk if they'd told her anything of great importance? Or even been suspected of telling her anything?

She remembered thinking that she had changed, become harder during her quest. And that people who had once known her might have a difficult time recognizing her now…as she might herself. She'd almost been proud of that fact. Then, by what almost seemed a miracle, she'd found something of her real self again on this vast and timeless land. About the same time as she'd found Quint.

Had it already been too late for the two of them by the time she'd arrived at the ranch and told her first lie? She'd achieved what she'd set out to do—to gain his trust. Only, once again, she hadn't concerned herself with the responsibility that gaining such trust brought with it. The obligation not to hurt the person who trusted you.

Katlin knew she'd hurt Quint. Most of his anger sprang from his feeling of betrayal.

She hadn't betrayed him, though! If she could just get him to see—

She buried her face in her hands and let the too-long contained tears flow.

There wasn't anything for it but to leave.

Maybe one day she could come back and they could start over....

She drew a quivering breath.

She'd arrived on the Parker Ranch with the secret idea that Quint would, in all likelihood, need to ask forgiveness from her. In fact, it had turned out that she needed to ask his forgiveness. She needed it from a lot of other people, as well. From everyone she might have hurt along the way.

KATLIN SLEPT after a long spell of crying. When she awakened some time later she checked Quint's trailer for lights. There were none.

She wanted desperately to see him again.

But being subjected to the cold anger she knew would be in his eyes, when such a short time before they'd been warm and welcoming, was more than she could presently take.

Her life had been in flux since Michael's death. She'd been so single-minded that she'd become a stranger to all the values she'd been raised with. She needed to go back home, to her parents. To tell them what she'd learned, but also to feel their gentle love as she mourned—in a way she'd never fully allowed herself to do before—all of life's might-have-beens.

Her bedside clock said it was a little after four in the morning.

She cried again as she wrote a short note on the back of the photo of her family. She wanted to leave it for Quint…she didn't know why. She just knew she wanted to do it. Possibly, to show him that Michael truly was her brother…in case he doubted even that from her lips.

After splashing her face with water, Katlin went outside. Using a small flashlight, she set the photo in a crack of the trailer's front door, then unhooked the electricity and water connections.

She paused for a final look around. She would remember this place forever.

And Quint.

Her gaze moved again over the dim outline of the trailer, then she climbed into the motor home, settled behind the wheel and started the engine.

Within seconds, she was on her way.

QUINT, AWAKENED from a troubled sleep, wasn't sure at first whether the sound he heard was left over from his dream or the real thing. When it continued, he realized the noise came from outside.

He jerked up and swept aside a short curtain. Katlin's motor home was heading toward the road!

He grabbed his jeans and hopped into them as he hurried to the door.

By the time he stepped outside, all he could see was taillights.

"No!" he heard himself cry out...somewhere between regret and protest.

But he didn't move.

He could get the pickup. Even going back inside for his jacket and boots, he could still catch up with her.

But he didn't move.

The metal door frame cut into his hands as he continued to grip it.

Then, when he could no longer see the taillights, he closed the door and went back to bed.

His heart hammered.

CHAPTER FOURTEEN

QUINT SLEPT SO LATE the next morning the horses had to call to him. He dragged himself out of bed and went to tend them, trying hard not to think of anything except what he was doing.

On his return to the trailer, his gaze unwillingly touched the empty space where Katlin's motor home had been parked. The extension cord and length of hose she'd borrowed were both coiled neatly on the ground. He steeled himself to go retrieve them.

He hadn't expected her to leave like that.

He put the hookups back in storage, and for good measure, rearranged a section of the shed that had needed straightening for a long time. Anything to keep busy.

Then, once again, he headed back to the trailer. He needed to eat something. His last meal had been at breakfast yesterday. With her. At the cabin. He immediately severed that line of thought. He didn't want to remember!

As he reached to open the door something fluttered against a metal chair leg, catching his attention. He bent to pick it up.

It was a photograph of four people on a beach.

One of them was Katlin. She was smiling, as were
the others—another woman, older, and a young man
whose arms rested across the two women's shoulders. A little to one side, a gray-haired man examined a shell he must have found at the water's edge.

Quint's gaze was drawn back to Katlin. She
looked the same and yet different, younger than in
mere years. Then his gaze went again to the man in
the middle. Well-set, handsome, in his early to mid
thirties. The last time Quint had seen him was when
he'd helplessly watched him die—Sergeant Michael
Brown.

Quint hadn't seen the similarity before because
he'd never seen Sergeant Brown smile. Quint flipped
the photo over, searching for…he didn't know what.
Names, a date. Anything to give him more information.

Script blossomed in a flowery hand.

My family as it used to be, Quint. I love them
more than I can say.

He read the words again. She'd been telling the
truth!

He brought the photo inside with him and collapsed into the recliner. He couldn't put the snapshot
down.

SOMETIME LATER the sound of an engine roused him
from his stupor. He blinked, thought for one im-

probable moment it might be her, then, on checking, confirmed that it wasn't. The visitor was Morgan, who strode across the yard from a ranch pickup.

Quint opened the trailer door before his cousin could knock and withstood his instant appraisal.

"Well, you look like hell," Morgan said, making no effort to sugarcoat his opinion as he stepped inside.

"Thanks," Quint said dryly.

"Mae sent me out here," Morgan said. "She wants to see you. This morning. No delay."

Quint rubbed a hand over his face and felt the lengthening stubble on his cheeks, chin and neck. "She's gonna have to wait until I get this off."

"I don't think she cares. She's hoppin'."

"Because Katlin left?" Quint asked.

Morgan narrowed his pale eyes. "Probably more because of *when* she left and *how*. Mae got word she took outta here like a scalded cat sometime before sunup."

"Great," Quint muttered.

"Mae wants to talk to you about it. I'm supposed to bring you in."

Quint's smile was wry. "Sounds like I'm going to a hanging—my own."

Morgan tipped his head. "What happened out here, Quint? Why'd she take off like that? When Christine and I visited everything seemed to be goin' just fine between you two."

"I'll get my hat," Quint said.

He took the snapshot to his bedroom and slipped it inside a drawer. Then he went back to accompany his cousin to the pickup.

"Want me to bring my own truck? Save you the drive back?" he offered.

"Mae said specifically I was to *bring* you in, so I don't think she'd appreciate it if I didn't."

Quint nodded and settled into the passenger seat.

As they pulled away from camp, his gaze went again to the space where the motor home had been. The emptiness matched exactly the emptiness he felt in his heart.

MAE PARKER SAW Quint alone in her office. She, too, subjected him to an appraisal, but her estimating look took longer, went deeper. It would have been enough to make him squirm if he hadn't been accustomed to giving a few of those "What the hell have you done now?" looks to subordinates during his years as an officer. He waited patiently for Mae to finish her attempt at intimidation.

"What's this I hear about Katlin Carter leavin' in the middle of the night? I sent her out to Big Spur because I thought I could trust you. Was I wrong in that?"

"No, ma'am, you weren't."

"Then why'd she leave?"

"I didn't tell her to. I didn't make her."

"Was it something you did?"

He hesitated. "No, ma'am."

Mae's hawklike eyes narrowed. "I think you'd better tell me, boy. I'm not going to let you outta here until you do. I mean to have an answer!"

Quint debated what to say. He'd never told anyone about what had happened, why he'd suddenly left the service. Never made excuses for himself, not even to his mother or his sister. And no one on the ranch had ever delved into it, respecting his privacy. But this time Mae was determined. And despite her advancing age, she was a fierce woman when she was determined about something.

"Her name isn't Katlin Carter," Quint said. "It's Katlin Brown. And she wasn't interested in writing about the vanishing Texas cowboy for *Eyes On Texas* magazine. She used that as a ploy to talk to me."

Mae's dark eyes gleamed. "I thought there was something funny goin' on. What did she want to talk to you about?"

"Something that happened while I was in the Army. It…concerned her brother."

"What about her brother?" Mae demanded, having duly noted his hesitation.

"He died. I was there. She thought I could tell her something."

"She told me she had a brother, but she didn't say he was dead. She told us a lot of things that didn't pan out, didn't she?"

"Yes, ma'am," Quint said tersely.

Mae's gaze flickered. As astute as she still was,

she knew he was holding back. But instead of questioning him further, she said, "I called *Eyes On Texas* magazine, you know, back when she first came here. The woman I talked to confirmed that Katlin Carter worked for them and planned to write a series of articles on the Texas cowboy. What do you think happened there? Did she get someone on the inside to speak up for her?"

"Possibly. She can be persuasive." He did his best to keep his tone level, making his reply an observation rather than a personal point of pain.

Mae's lips tightened. "Well, that makes me madder than all get-out! I don't like bein' lied to. And particularly not by someone who's only doin' it to get on this ranch! I think I'm going to call this Malcolm Thompson—he's the magazine's Chief Editor, or so it says on his letter. I suppose it's his letter." She closely checked the signature on the correspondence she pulled from a desk drawer. "I think I'm goin' to give him a little piece of my mind. I wrote down the young lady's name who confirmed Miss Carter's identity, as well. In my opinion, she should be dismissed. But most of all, I think Mr. Thompson needs to know about what this Katlin—Brown, did you say?—has been doin' in the name of his magazine. Maybe he'd like to file some kind of charge with the authorities. Surely, there's something he could do."

"Her brother died, Mae. She was only trying to find out how it happened. She and her parents weren't given a lot of information. You can't blame her for that, can you?'' Quint knew how strongly Mae Parker felt about family. He was sure the argument would carry weight.

The high degree of alarm he'd felt for Katlin as Mae spoke angrily of retribution surprised him. Yet he also had another consideration—he didn't want his part in the misrepresentation to become known and possibly draw unwanted attention. Particularly the attention of a widely distributed magazine's chief editor. He'd given up so much. It *couldn't* be for nothing. The true story couldn't get out!

''So you're sayin' you don't think I should call him,'' Mae stated, then was silent a moment. ''There's something else you're not tellin' me, but I'm not about to get it out of you, am I?''

''No, ma'am,'' he answered promptly.

''Probably *more* than one something. Like the story behind how you found out who this Katlin person really is.''

When he didn't answer, she sat looking at him for a long time. Then, nodding as if she'd somehow confirmed her own speculation, she said, ''Okay. I won't complain. To Malcom Thompson or to anyone. Like you said, she's lost a brother. Something like that can make a person behave pretty strangely.''

Quint shifted, ready to get back to Big Spur.

Mae didn't release him. ''You look rough. You gonna be all right?''

"Yes, ma'am. I'm fine."

"You eatin'?"

"When I want."

"Maybe you'd better pick up a few more supplies to take back with you. Tell Axel I said to give you some extra meat and eggs."

"Thank you, ma'am."

Mae smiled. A smile Quint wasn't sure he'd ever seen before. He wasn't accustomed to such solicitousness from her. He decided he must look pretty bad.

WHEN MORGAN discovered that Quint had yet to eat breakfast, he insisted that they stop by Little Springs so his mother or Christine could correct the oversight.

Shortly after, they left with Quint sated both in food and in care. Morgan must have warned them, because no one mentioned his missing visitor.

On the way back to Big Spur the cousins' fitful conversation concentrated on the weather and ranch work. Only as Morgan dropped off Quint did they return to the reason for Mae's summons.

"I may be puttin' my nose in where it doesn't belong," Morgan chanced to say. "But after we left here last time for our picnic, Christine told me you two might be a little more interested in each other than it looked on the surface. She's pretty good with that kinda thing. So I believed her. Now I can't help but wonder if that might have somethin' to do with why Katlin took off the way she did. You gonna tell me whether I'm right?''

Quint kept his features bland, knowing that Morgan's keen ex-lawman instincts had been activated. ''Nope,'' he answered shortly.

Morgan slanted a smile. ''Well, I guess that makes it clear as mud.''

''Not much to tell,'' Quint said, softening his refusal.

''You noticed she was pretty…I saw that, remember?''

''Have to be blind not to notice.''

''That's what I thought.''

Quint slapped the roof of the pickup by way of dismissal. ''Won't keep you,'' he said.

Morgan still didn't budge. ''Christine would want me to tell you something. By way of a little piece of advice. If, after a while, you still miss her, it might not be a bad idea to go look her up. Don't worry about your time. I'll square it.''

''Thanks,'' Quint answered gruffly, then waved as his cousin finally set the pickup in motion and circled back onto the narrow graded road.

QUINT WAS TOO RESTLESS not to work. He saddled Chili and rode out into the pasture.

''Had yourself a little vacation, didn't you, boy?'' he murmured to the horse. ''She didn't make you work hard. But it's back to business now. Vacation's over,'' he added as they went after a calf to separate it from its mother.

Once they'd finished and the calf scampered away, Quint and Chili rode on.

As the afternoon lengthened and silence settled over him, Quint found that he missed having her ride along.

Which was a complete contradiction to what he'd felt before.

But then everything in his life seemed to revolve around some kind of contradiction. His father loving his mother, yet putting the Army first. His own desire to be a soldier, to follow in his father's footsteps, yet loving to be on his own, tending cattle. His being a soldier—a philosophy of life so completely at odds with being a cowboy that it was almost laughable. A soldier was always told what to do, and was even given a manual on exactly how to do it. A cowboy accepted being told what needed to be done, but heaven help the person who crossed the unseen line and told the cowboy how to go about doing it. A soldier followed each and every order. A cowboy lived to be free, proud of being his own man.

Then there was this thing with Katlin. At the start, he hadn't wanted her to be at Big Spur. Now he found himself missing all the questions she asked. Missing her smile. Missing...her.

Earlier, Mae had said something that resonated.

Something about how he'd learned who "this Katlin person" really was.

When he thought back to what had been said last night, he had to acknowledge that he'd learned who she was because *she'd* volunteered the information. He hadn't "found her out." He still wouldn't be any the wiser if she hadn't told him.

It hurt too much to think about for very long, because although she'd told him the truth about who she was, everything she'd done, everything she'd said since her arrival in Big Spur had been geared to gain information about her brother.

As he'd accused her of doing and she had not denied, she'd been willing to do *anything*. Even pretend that she cared for him.

THE NOISE of the busy terminal in San Francisco assaulted Katlin as she made her way to a taxi to take her home. But even in the taxi, a cacophony of sounds assailed her. Horns blew, truck engines rumbled, tires hummed over the roadway and rattled over so-called repairs. The common din of everyday life in a metropolitan area.

As Quint had said, the hardest thing to get used to after spending time on the ranch was the noise people made in the outside world. She understood completely what he meant now, even after just a week.

A pang of regret shot through her—for what she'd said and done, for what she'd not said and not done.

Maybe there would have been another way if she'd thought longer, harder, less selfishly.

After leaving the ranch she'd driven straight through to the West Texas oil center of Odessa, returned the rented motor home, then taken a shuttle to the airport, where she caught the first plane she could to the west coast.

Like a wounded animal, she sought safety and shelter. She needed her parents possibly more than she'd ever needed them before.

She felt as if she'd lost her way.

She carried with her a truth, though. At least, enough of a truth to offer them relief.

The home she'd grown up in was tucked into a hillside overlooking a narrow valley, where the center of the tiny town below hugged the edge of a busy freeway. The house was high enough that sound was muted, and when Katlin stepped out of the taxi to be met with the scents of junipers and flowers and braced by the relatively cooler air, she sighed at that harmonious contribution to solace. Then she walked up the short curving path to the front door.

Her hands trembled as she used the brass knocker. Calling up her last bit of determination, she controlled her emotions. She didn't want to burst into tears the instant she saw either of her parents.

But that was exactly what happened. When Deborah Brown opened the door, looked shocked, then instantly overjoyed to see her, Katlin could no longer hold on. Huge tears sprang from her eyes even as her chin quivered, and she cast herself into her mother's waiting arms.

"Katlin?" Deborah murmured, surprised by the uncharacteristic display. Then, shushing and crooning soft words of comfort, her mother closed them into the privacy of the house.

When Adam Brown came to see what was happening, he made a startled sound and immediately joined the embrace.

They stood there, a united trio, until Katlin could pull herself together.

Smiling her love, Katlin's mother supplied her with a handful of tissues to dry her eyes and her nose, after which her father saw her to a soft leather couch.

"We had no idea you were coming," her father said. "Why didn't you call? We'd've met you at the airport. You don't look—you look as if you could have done with a hug right away."

Katlin smiled and sniffed and dabbed at remaining wet spots. "I didn't know I was coming today. I just…took the first flight here."

"Would you like a cup of tea, sweetheart? Your father and I were just about to have one. Have you eaten? We have some leftover chicken from dinner and a huge fruit salad I made for tomorrow."

"Some tea, yes. Nothing else, though. I—I ate on the plane." She'd eaten a few crackers on the last leg of the journey. "I…It was crackers. I'm not very hungry.'' She was tired of lies. *So* tired of lies. She never wanted to utter another falsehood!

Her mother's glance went over her. ''Just a little toast to go with your tea,'' she urged. ''Something light. Think that might hit the spot?''

''Thanks, Mom,'' Katlin said.

Deborah went happily to see to the nourishment, while Adam stayed at Katlin's side.

''We're glad to have you home, sweetheart,'' he said.

Katlin knew he wanted to ask why she'd turned up so precipitously, but he held back.

''Dad, there's something I have to tell you and Mom.''

''Are you getting married?'' he asked calmly.

Katlin started. ''No.''

''Were you planning to get married and it didn't work out?''

''Dad, I don't understand. Where did you get the idea that I—''

''Young women don't usually come running home as upset as you are if it doesn't involve a man.''

An image of Quint popped immediately into Katlin's mind. She wanted to contradict her father's statement, but couldn't when he was mostly right.

Her father smiled. ''Now don't deny that there's a man you're having problems with. Tell me who he is and I'll go beat him up!''

The idea that her sweet gentle father would rush

to beat up anyone made Katlin laugh unsteadily. "It's not that. Well, it is, sort of. There's a lot I have to explain to you, Dad. To you and Mom both."

The term "explain" was difficult for her, coming so freshly on the heels of her use of it last night. Had it *only* been last night? She felt in a different world again. Her, here on the Pacific Coast; Quint, in the back of beyond in West Texas. All the miles in between could be a yawning chasm that might never be bridged.

Her father patted her nervous hands. "Have your tea and toast first, soak in a nice warm bath, hop into your gown, then we'll have a little talk after you're in bed. You look as if you could sleep for two days straight."

KATLIN'S ROOM was as she'd left it several years ago. In reality, as she'd left it after graduating high school. She'd removed most of her "baby" things before leaving for college. She'd wanted so badly then to be seen as an adult. Only a few things remained from her earlier years—a plush rabbit that had been with her since she was five, a poster of a pop group Michael had sent her from overseas and, knowing that she was a fan, gone backstage to have the group members autograph. It had been the envy of all her friends. A couple of ribbons for high placement in math contests. But in place of honor, never ever considered when she discarded things, was a studio photo of Michael in his Army uniform. He looked so young—he'd been in his early twenties, younger than she was now—his expression alive with expectation and pride.

Ahh, Michael, she thought as she curled up on the foot of the bed, her gown tucked beneath her knees, *I hope you found someone to love.* And she was startled by the realization that the idea had never occurred to her before. She had no idea whether Michael had left a girlfriend behind. Or several girlfriends. She'd always looked at him as some kind of special superhero, without a real life beyond his familiar uniform.

A light tap sounded on her door and her parents came through when she called to them.

"You look better," her mother said, coming to kiss her softly on top of her head.

"I couldn't sleep on the plane. I napped, but—" She shrugged.

Her mother took a place opposite her on the foot of the bed. Her father settled in a chair, which he scooted closer.

"Now," he said, indulgently. "What's this you have to explain?"

Almost an exact repetition of Quint's words! Katlin's courage faltered. Would they want to hear what she had to tell them when she had nothing to back it up but Quint's word? That was good enough for her, because she knew the quiet strength of his character. He wouldn't have said what he did about

Michael if it hadn't been true, even though he'd refused point-blank to expand on his statement. Would it be a kindness to make them revisit their sadness over Michael's death? Or would her knowing the truth be enough?

She examined her parents with the wisdom of a newly reached maturity...and saw that the pain was still there.

She took a breath. "I know you've wondered why I've been away so much for the past couple of years..." she began, and told them everything.

Katlin told them about the way she'd carried on her quest to learn the truth about Michael's death, about the reason she'd needed the flexibility of temporary jobs, about hearing of Captain Quinton McCabe and tracing him to Texas, about moving to Texas and locating him on a ranch through her researcher's job at the magazine, about going to the ranch and meeting him under false pretenses.

She spared herself nothing. She confessed how she'd deceived and maneuvered people, how she'd used them for her own ends. Then she told them what Quint had said.

"The accident *wasn't* Michael's fault! He didn't do anything to cause it. Or to cause him and the other soldiers to lose their lives. Quint said the officer who came to visit you was mistaken."

Her parents looked thunderstruck.

"Quint was positive about what he said," she

continued. "And I believe him. He isn't the sort of man to— *We* can believe him," she finished huskily.

Her mother whispered, "Michael didn't—?" and tears suddenly welled in her eyes. She couldn't go on.

Adam Brown swallowed thickly. When he spoke his voice was gruff. "And this Captain McCabe…he would have been in a position to know?"

Katlin had already filled in that particular blank, but her father must have either missed it, or he needed added reassurance.

"He was there," Katlin repeated. "He wouldn't talk about it, but he—he—"

Adam stood and reached for Deborah, who cried silently. He folded her into his embrace. "I never really believed—" he began, then stopped. All present knew what he'd been about to say and concurred.

"It must have been hard for you," Deborah said, extending a hand to press her daughter's fingers.

"It was harder *not* to know," Katlin answered.

"I can't believe…. Why would someone say that about Michael? I don't understand," Deborah said.

Adam met Katlin's gaze, and for the first time, she saw anger and resentment flash in his eyes.

"I assured Quint I wasn't out to make trouble for anyone," she said quickly.

"I'd like to make trouble for him!" her father bit out.

"Not for Quint! It wasn't him. He didn't know what we'd been told."

"I meant, make trouble for the officer who came here. The man who said what he did about Michael!" Then, though delayed, her quick defense of the man she'd quoted made her father's expression switch from anger to speculation. "This Quint McCabe...you say he's a cowboy?"

"He is now."

"What kind of cowboy?"

Katlin laughed unsteadily. "The kind who tends cattle on a ranch in West Texas."

"Is that *all* he is?" her father asked.

Katlin knew he was again putting the pieces together and coming up with a correct answer. Her determination to be finished with lies and evasions left her with nothing to say. She couldn't deny that Quint had played a major role in her headlong rush home.

Her continued silence soon attracted her mother's attention, too.

"A *cowboy?*" Deborah echoed, as if the breed was already long extinct.

CHAPTER FIFTEEN

As ADAM BROWN had predicted, Katlin slept through the night and for a large portion of the next day. She'd been exhausted, but the depletion had gone beyond physical tiredness. She might have been sleeping away the vestiges of the past three years.

When she awakened she no longer felt a heavy sense of obligation. She'd fulfilled the duty she'd set for herself. She'd rid Michael's memory of the uncertainty surrounding his death and, in the process, confirmed her deep belief that he had done nothing wrong.

She slipped out of bed, dressed in a pair of jeans and a shirt—clothes she'd brought with her from Texas—and went downstairs. She found her mother in the kitchen, puttering. The instant Deborah saw Katlin, she hurried over.

As in the days when Katlin was a small girl, her mother brushed flyaway hairs from her face as an excuse to examine her.

"You look much better, sweetheart. Much better. Your father will be so relieved. He didn't want to go to work today, but he had a meeting he couldn't put off…and I told him he should go. You'd want him to.''

''Yes, definitely.'' Katlin checked the wall clock. ''Especially since I've slept most of the day away.''

It was three o'clock. Five o'clock on the Parker Ranch. Quint was probably still out riding pasture. She shook her head to clear the thought.

''You needed the rest,'' Deborah said simply.

Noting her mother's freshly prepared cup of tea, Katlin made her own cup and took it to the table. It felt odd to suddenly have so much room to work.

Deborah settled at the table as well, but instead of continuing the conversation, she grew quiet. Then finally, huskily, she said, ''I'm so glad to have you home.''

''It hasn't been that long, Mom.''

''It *feels* that long.'' Deborah struggled to brighten. ''But no, you're right. It hasn't been that long. And, after all, you were in Texas.''

''Yes.''

''Are you…planning to go back?''

Katlin considered her answer. Her original plan had been to return to Arlington to settle things before returning to California. But that plan had been made before her emotions had become so entangled. Yesterday, she just hadn't thought. ''I still have an apartment.''

''What about your job at the magazine?''

''I quit.''

''You did?''

"It had served its purpose, Mom."

Deborah nodded, but Katlin could see that the full import of everything she'd done in Texas over the past six months was still a little muddled in her mother's mind. She'd been existing in a fog for so long; it was going to take her time to adjust.

"So," Katlin completed, "I guess I should go back...to release the apartment and get my things. The apartment came furnished and everything else should fit in my car. I should say a few goodbyes, too."

"Is one of them to your cowboy?"

"He's in West Texas, Mom."

"Don't you have to drive through western Texas to get here from Arlington?"

"I—" Katlin hadn't thought of that. "Not... necessarily. I can take another route."

Her mother frowned. "But I thought you'd *want* to see him."

Katlin crossed to the French doors that opened onto the garden deck. Oh, she wanted to see him. Only, was he ready to see her?

Instead of addressing her mother's assumption, she said, "I wonder...could I come stay with you and Dad for a while? I'm not sure what I'll be doing from now on. Everything's so—I just don't know."

Deborah came to stand beside her. "Of course, you can. It will be like having our little girl back again."

"I'm not a little girl, Mom," Katlin said quietly.

"You'll always be our little girl. Just like Michael—Michael will always be our little boy. Although, I don't think of him so much as a little boy anymore. I almost always remember him a hefty six-footer, with that great big smile." Her voice caught, wavered. "I wish he could come home, too."

Pain infused her mother's words, but at least she was talking about Michael again. For too long, she'd kept silent, holding her sorrow inside.

"I dreamed about him the other night," Katlin murmured.

"I did, too!" her mother exclaimed, looking surprised.

"Did he say anything to you?" Katlin asked.

Her mother hesitated. "He said everything was going to be all right. Then he left." She looked at Katlin. "Do you think he might have known what you were doing?"

Katlin's throat had grown too tight for words. She nodded. And the two women leaned toward each other, their arms locking, as if Michael stood behind them, hugging them, just as he used to.

WHEN QUINT SETTLED on a course of action he saw it through.

Only now he had the added complication of whether to set another wrong right and by so doing, chance exposure of the secret he carried for the Colonel.

The choices were at total odds to each other.

If he did nothing, the Browns would continue to suffer doubt about Michael's actions at the time of his death, even though Quint had witnessed the other man's heroism. And if he told the Browns everything that he, in good conscience, could about the mission, word might get out, smearing the Colonel's record and leaving Agnes to suffer. He would also be contravening the secrecy clause he'd agreed to when he resigned.

He could be assured that Katlin would tell her parents what he'd told her, but how much good would that do, when all he'd said was that the officer who'd visited them was mistaken? That didn't constitute a lot of reassurance.

Then there was Katlin herself. If he'd been placed in the same position, wouldn't he have been willing to say or do whatever it took to separate fact from fiction? She'd said her parents' lives had been torn apart. Wasn't she, in a slightly different way, only doing what he'd done for the Colonel? She'd spent years, she'd said, trying to find the answer. And he hadn't believed her. Not until he saw the beach snapshot. And even then…he'd been wounded, thinking she'd deceived him.

She'd denied it, telling him that she'd been caught as much by surprise by the attraction between them as he had been.

Which was true…he had been surprised.

And still was…judging by the degree of pain he felt at her deception. But he was also surprised by his growing belief that he'd been wrong to doubt her—that she really meant what she'd said.

Days had passed with all these thoughts doing battle in his head. Not even a trip to the plateau rim had settled his mind.

A good soldier would leave things as they were. The military and everyone else involved wanted to forget Manzant, to pretend that it never happened. He'd accepted that and used it for his own purpose for the Colonel. Because of the Colonel he also didn't want the mission to be investigated.

But…how could he leave things as they were?

How could he allow himself to let Katlin go?

He couldn't even stop thinking about her!

QUINT MADE HIS DECISION and drove to the Hugheses to use their telephone.

He called every person named *Brown* in Lafayette, California, and none of them had a family member by the name of Katlin or Michael. He called *Eyes On Texas* magazine, and all he could get the personnel officer to divulge was that Katlin Brown was no longer employed by the company. He called the Information service for the entire Dallas/Fort Worth area and no one by her name had a listed number.

His frustration was mounting when he remembered that Mae had said she'd written down the name of the woman at the magazine who'd vouched for Katlin. So he called Mae and got the name.

He didn't care who knew he was trying to locate Katlin or the Browns. His aunt Delores, who'd been unable to avoid hearing his part of the various conversations since only the two of them were in the house, had seemed startled at first, then pleased as she realized that Quint had "found himself a woman friend," as she'd put it. And that the woman was the visitor from the magazine they'd all spent time speculating about both before her arrival and after her abrupt departure.

Quint knew his determination to find Katlin would be all over the ranch by nightfall. But that did nothing to stop him. He called Tessa Goodall and, loading his requests with steely persistence, wrung the truth out of her. She gave him Katlin's phone number in Arlington, as well as the actual name of the town in California where Katlin had grown up and where her parents currently resided. And she'd even told him how she'd helped Katlin because Katlin had told her *he* owed her money.

Another lie. To achieve her purpose.

Quint was unswayed. After several failed attempts to reach her in Arlington, his next call was to the airline where he reserved a seat on a plane going west that night.

"I'm good for whatever those calls end up costing," Quint assured his aunt, once he'd finished.

"I know that!" Delores retorted. "Do I need to tell Morgan you're gonna be off a while?"

"I'll find him and tell him myself. Need to bring the horses in, too."

Delores nodded. "We've got room. He'll take real good care of 'em for you." She paused and asked, "You want me to wish you good luck?"

"I'm probably going to need more than luck, Aunt Delores."

"Whatever it is, just tell her you're sorry," his aunt teased. "That always puts a woman in a better frame of mind."

"I'll remember that," Quint said, then smiling, kissed her cheek.

IN ALL HIS TRAVELS Quint had never been to the San Francisco Bay Area. After he arrived he found a place to stay for the rest of the night—a hotel not far from the airport—then the next morning, drove the rental car to the East Bay and the appointment he'd made with the Browns.

When he'd asked for Katlin, the man who answered—her father—had told him she was out of town. Quint's heart had grown heavier, but her presence wasn't necessary. In fact, in one way, Quint knew he'd find it easier to talk with her parents if she wasn't there. It was going to be hard enough to do what he had to do, without the added complication of his confused feelings for her.

The beauty of the area lived up to all the hype, Quint decided as he drove along the freeways. The city itself was a jewel on the tip of a peninsula. The low hills and mountains that bordered the bay opposite the city were filled with houses, businesses and schools. The place teemed with people and yet, at the same time, nature still held sway. The populace would have to pave the place over before it could possibly be thought of as ugly.

Quint drove into a long tunnel bored through a mountain and exited at the first town. He saw on the map and highway signs that Lafayette was the next town on—Katlin had at least stuck close to the truth when she told him it was her home.

A short time later he drew up in front of the house. The area had a rugged beauty different from West Texas. The hills, folding into themselves, were smoother, rounder, and carpeted with golden grass. A multitude of houses clung to the hillsides. *Very* different from West Texas.

Quint set his shoulders and walked to the door.

The man who answered his knock was right at six foot, in his early sixties, with a full head of gray hair and strongly formed features. His gaze was level, curious and quite a bit suspicious.

"Mr. Brown?" Quint asked.

"Adam Brown," the man said.

Quint extended his hand and the man took it. Then he invited Quint inside.

The interior of the house was about what Quint would have expected. Roomy and furnished with good taste and a healthy wallet...it also looked comfortable, lived-in. A family home of long standing.

"Will Mrs. Brown be joining us?" Quint asked as he sat down on the leather couch.

"I thought it best that the two of us meet on our own," Adam Brown answered quietly. "You said this was about...Michael?"

"Yes, sir." Quint appreciated the man's desire to shield his wife. "I met your daughter, Katlin, recently and she told me what you'd been told about your son. I thought it time to set the record straight."

"I thought you'd already done that. Katlin told us what you said. That the officer was wrong in what he led us to believe."

"Yes, sir. He was wrong."

The older man's eyes moved over him. "You're not what I expected."

"What did you expect?"

"A cowboy. You look like a businessman...like me."

"I'm a cowboy who owns a business suit."

Adam Brown grinned slightly, then waited.

Quint knew it was over to him. He took a breath. "Your son was a hero, Mr. Brown. He didn't cause anything tragic to happen. We were on a mission, we came under fire, your son—Michael—was trying to help pull a wounded man on board the helicopter when he was hit. He didn't have to put himself at risk, but he did. That's how he died. Trying to save someone else."

Adam Brown was very still. Then he, too, drew

a breath. It took a moment before he spoke again. Finally, he said, "Then why were we told differently?"

Quint studied his hands for a moment before looking up. "What I'm telling you, Mr. Brown, is classified. The entire mission is classified. There are things I won't tell you because I can't. What I've already told you is enough to put me in prison for a number of years, just for talking with you about it. I didn't know your son, Mr. Brown. We met that day. Just like I met everyone else that day. I can't tell you where we went or what we did there. I also can't answer why the officer who visited you said what he did. My first suspicion is that he was given the assignment to keep things quiet, and that's the route he chose. Either he didn't think or didn't care what it might do to you and your family. I doubt the order to tell you Michael was at fault came from higher up."

"I'd like to find out!"

"I don't blame you," Quint said honestly. "I'd feel the same."

Adam Brown stood up and paced across the room. When he turned back he said, "I understand what you've said, Mr. McCabe, and I appreciate you coming all this way to say it. But I'm still left to wonder why you waited until now."

"I didn't know before."

"You only learned what we were told when Katlin told you."

"Yes, sir."

"Why didn't you tell her?"

Quint was silent.

Adam Brown looked at him with even more curiosity and, once again, waited.

"I had to think, to consider," Quint said. "This involves more than just me. Like I said, I could go to jail. But more importantly, the reputation of a man I highly respected—a loyal friend of my father's and of my family, who had a stroke shortly after the mission and later died—is at stake. If this were to come out—I'll do everything I can to protect his memory and to protect his wife. I've *done* everything I can. But I can't stand by and let your son's reputation be damaged in your eyes. The Colonel wouldn't want me to, neither would my father."

The older man studied him. "I can see where this has been difficult."

"Yes, sir."

"Not to mention the added complication of my daughter," Adam Brown accurately guessed.

"Yes, sir. That, too."

The man came to stand in front of him. "You didn't have to do what you did, Mr. McCabe. You didn't have to come here. You didn't have to tell Katlin even the little that you did. You didn't have to tell me more." He paused. "There's nothing to be gained by taking this any further. It won't bring Michael back or the other two men, and will only cause problems for you and your Colonel. He must have been quite a man to deserve such loyalty. Rest assured,'' he said, extending his hand, ''this will go no further than my wife and my daughter. We're the only ones who were hurt by this and the only ones who'll appreciate what you've done. Michael would approve, I'm sure.''

''Thank you, sir,'' Quint said.

''Call me Adam.''

''Call me Quint.''

Adam lifted an eyebrow. ''Now, I suppose you'd like me to tell you where Katlin is. Well, she's back in Texas, packing her things, to drive back here. Her phone's already been disconnected, and she could be starting off at any time. She also said something about saying goodbye to friends. So she could be longer. She'll probably give us a call along the way and, eventually, turn up. You still have our number?''

''I do.''

''Use it whenever you want.''

AS KATLIN GATHERED her things in the living room of her apartment in Arlington, she found that she'd acquired more possessions than she'd thought during her six months living in the state. After a quick weed out, she brought the extras along with her when she met Tessa Goodall that evening. Tessa had sounded a little strained when they'd spoken on the phone last night, but Katlin had put that down to some sort of stress at work. Malcolm Thompson should still be in Tahiti but that didn't mean problems wouldn't crop up.

Katlin parked the car where she could see it from inside the restaurant. When Tessa arrived, Katlin was happy to greet her. Tessa was one of the few friends she'd let herself make during her sojourn at the magazine.

Only the strain Katlin felt from her over the telephone had increased. Tessa, normally vibrant and funny and ready to chatter about anything, held back, unsmiling. Katlin frowned. She hoped her actions hadn't caused trouble for her at work.

"Is something wrong?" Katlin asked. "You seem…upset."

All Tessa needed was the opening. "Well, yes, I'm upset! This man called…the man you said owed you money. He told me he'd never met you before. And that I could be in a lot of trouble for helping you get on the Parker Ranch. That Mae Parker was angry, but he'd talked her out of calling Mr. Thompson to complain."

Katlin blinked. "Quint McCabe?"

"Yes, him. Did you lie to me, Katlin? Did you make it all up?" Tessa's anger had evolved into hurt. She looked ready to cry.

Katlin had wanted to tell her the truth herself. It was the main reason for this meeting. But now she had to grapple with Quint's call.

"What did he want?" she asked.

"I asked you first."

"Yes. I made it up. I needed your help and I thought that would be the only way to get you to do it. I'm sorry, Tessa. I'm sorry for lying and sorry that you had to hear it from someone else."

Tessa shuffled in her seat, then mollified, said, "All right, I'll forgive you. This time. Do you still want to know what he said?"

Katlin nodded, her stomach fluttering.

"He wanted me to give him your phone number, then he wanted to know how to get in touch with your parents."

"And you told him?"

"I had to. He was…determined. And he'd said Mae Parker was angry. I don't want her to call Mr. Thompson. He'd fire me!"

"Did he say he was going to call my parents?"

"He just said 'thanks' and hung up. I never heard from him again." She reached out to clasp Katlin's hand. "I didn't know what else to do. And…I was hurt."

"It's okay. Don't worry."

"But you look so pale!"

"Ah…listen. If it's all right with you, can we skip dinner and just put the things in your car? I—I have to go back to my apartment."

Tessa was already on her feet. "Of course. Is there anything I can do to help?"

Katlin tried to smile normally. "No. It's fine, Tessa. I can handle it. It's just…a misunderstanding."

Katlin's nerves were unsettled as she steered the car back to the apartment where she planned to stay overnight. That was when she remembered her telephone had already been disconnected.

She changed course into the nearest service station, hurried to the telephone box and dialed her parents' number.

"Katlin?" her father answered when she'd uttered an urgent "Dad?"

"Dad, it's me. I'm still in Arlington. Ah—have you received any calls from Quint McCabe?"

"I certainly have," her father said.

Katlin tightened her grip on the receiver. "What did he want?"

"Well, to see you. But to see us, too."

"What about?"

"I can't tell you on the phone. He flew out, we talked…and I have to say, I admire the young man."

"He flew out?" Katlin repeated, shocked.

"He was here today. Just left a few hours ago."

"Where was he going?"

"Back to the ranch, I guess. I didn't know how to tell him to get in touch with you."

"Back to—" she repeated. She couldn't believe Quint had left the ranch in the first place.

"I got the impression he really wants to talk to you, sweetheart. And if you feel anything for him…"

"I don't know what I feel, Dad." All her uncertainty was revealed in her voice.

"Then don't you think it might be a good idea to find out?"

KATLIN'S FATHER'S WORDS rang in her thoughts as she completed the short trip to her apartment, curled up on the couch and waited for morning.

Instinct urged her to leave right then. To drive through the night and present herself at the ranch early tomorrow morning.

But she controlled the impulse.

She'd been living by her wits for such a long time.

She no longer needed to do that.

If she was going to talk to Quint—as he obviously now wanted—she didn't want to rush into the moment.

It was too important.

CHAPTER SIXTEEN

KATLIN DIDN'T DRIVE straight to Big Spur. Instead, after leaving the motel where she'd spent the night, she stopped in front of the main house in the Parker Family compound.

She hadn't called ahead for an appointment because she had an idea Mae Parker would refuse to see her, and she didn't want to be rebuffed. She was determined to apologize for her deception.

The door opened immediately. Mae Parker herself stood like a sentinel in the entryway, unwilling to let her pass.

"Good morning," Katlin said as she stepped onto the porch displaying none of the Terylin Murphy arrogance and bravado. She extended her hand, but, as she expected, it was refused.

Mae Parker glared at her. "What do you want?"

"I came to offer you an apology. What I did was wrong. I'd like to give you my reason, though, and possibly then, you'll understand."

"I'll never understand a bald-faced lie."

"As I said, I had a reason. May I come in?"

There was no softening of the woman's expression. "You ate a meal under this roof in false pretense. I trusted you enough to let you spend time on the ranch. What do you want now? Must be somethin'.''

"I want to talk to you. And I want to talk to Quint."

"Don't you think you've done enough to Quint?"

"I didn't—"

Mae raised a quelling hand and looked her up and down. "All right," she said after a moment. "Come in. But you better be careful what you say. I don't like to be fooled. And anybody who tries it a second time is in deep trouble."

"I won't lie again," Katlin promised.

Mae's hawklike eyes sent her a show-me look, but she stepped aside and ushered Katlin into her office.

The woman settled behind her desk in the familiar room, leaving Katlin to choose whether she stood or sat. Katlin continued to stand.

"The last time I was here I told you I had a brother. I let you believe he was living in California, when, in reality, he died in a military accident that my parents and I were led to believe was his fault. I tried to get more information, but couldn't…until someone gave me Quint's name. They said he—that I should talk to him. I knew you wouldn't allow me just to come on the ranch, and I doubted he'd willingly agree to cooperate. So I devised a plan."

"You didn't think telling me the truth would work? It didn't occur to you that I might help?"

"I couldn't take that chance. If I told you the truth and you refused to let me see Quint, I didn't know how else to get to him. He was hidden so completely in Big Spur."

"And you learned this…how?" Mae inquired.

"I truly did work at *Eyes On Texas* magazine, but as a researcher, not a writer. I found some old articles about the ranch and asked a number of very judicious questions. I was left in little doubt about the power of the Parkers."

"Then it took some guts for you to do what you did."

"I had to find out."

"And did you?"

"Quint told me the accident wasn't Michael's fault."

"Why'd you leave so sudden-like if he told you what you needed? Why run away? In the dark, in a hurry. One of the cowboys saw you leave."

"That's…between me and Quint."

"Does he want to talk to you?"

"He just visited my parents in California. I wasn't there, but my father told me he wants to see me."

As their conversation progressed, the layers of Mae's anger peeled away. Finally, gruffly, she suggested, "Why don't you sit down? Have you been drivin' a long time?"

"I spent the night in Pecos." She named a town some hours north.

"Would you like something to eat, to drink?"

"No, ma'am. I just want to see Quint."

Mae was quiet, then she said, "I knew somethin' was up—that you were holding somethin' back—remember? I guessed it involved Quint when you insisted on going to Big Spur. I just couldn't figure out what it was, except that maybe it had something to do with him quittin' the Army. He's too young to wall himself off like he's been doing. I thought you might shake him up a little and get him out and about again. I thought it would be good for him. Only I wasn't countin' on you shakin' him up quite so much!"

Katlin agreed unsteadily. "I wasn't expecting it either."

Mae smiled, a short pull of her lips. "Sounds like maybe I shouldn't hold you up, then."

"I truly do apologize."

"Accepted. Now get going. I know he went right back to Big Spur after collecting the horses from Little Springs."

Katlin cocked her head. "So you already knew he went to California?"

Mae smiled again, only with more satisfaction. "There's not a lot goes on around here that I *don't* know about."

MAE SAW HER OFF with a waggle of her cane tip. Katlin waved in return, but Mae was already on her way back inside.

Katlin sighed as she pulled out of the U-shaped

drive. The first part of the ordeal was over. Now on to the next. As hard as it had been to talk to Mae, what followed would likely be far more difficult.

The butterflies in her stomach flapped like eagles by the time she'd made her way to the end of the graded road. An undercurrent of excitement hummed through her, yet, at the same time, so did trepidation.

She stepped out of her car at Big Spur and looked around. A horse in the far corral trotted over to the rails to see who'd arrived—Chili! She wanted to go to him, but held back.

Cupping her hands to her mouth as Morgan had done, she called, "Quint? Are you here?"

When she received no reply, she went to greet Chili. He seemed genuinely pleased to see her.

"Are they out working today, boy?" she asked. "I guess they are. But no matter, I'll wait."

She smiled when Chili dipped his head. He might have been showing concurrence. Then she went to sit under the awning. She would wait…for however long it took.

QUINT DISTRIBUTED salt licks to several pastures. Between the hard rain and animal use, the supply in place was mostly depleted. He fixed a little fence, doctored a cow, then started back to camp early. He could do more—there was always an endless supply of things that needed attention—but he couldn't stop thinking of Katlin. Where she might be. What she might be doing. If she'd contacted her parents yet.

Her father had said to call. So, that's what he planned to do. Later, he'd take a quick run back to Little Springs and use his aunt and uncle's phone again.

But as he neared camp, he saw a sporty red car parked at the edge of the clearing. He pulled Jim up, frowning. Who? Then he saw her sitting under the awning in one of his old metal chairs...and his heart gave a springing leap. *Katlin!*

He could barely believe what he saw. She was here!

Only then did the full impact of his years of isolation hit him. He'd been alone, but he'd never realized how lonely he'd been. He'd let himself drift, his life on hold...almost as if he were doing penance for the lives of the three men the Army had held him accountable for losing. As if, since he'd shouldered the blame, he should feel guilt.

But he wasn't guilty. He'd done nothing wrong! No more than any of the others on that helicopter.

He was no more responsible for what had occurred that night than Michael Brown had been.

He urged Jim forward and watched, narrow-eyed, as she spotted them and stood up.

KATLIN KEPT her arms tightly at her sides, quelling the urge to run to him.

Quint and Jim moved forward slowly. He'd seen

her before she'd seen him. They came right up to the awning before Quint slipped out of the saddle.

"You're back," he said.

His voice, his face...everything about him!... thrilled her to her core.

"Yes," she said.

His pale eyes moved over her. She'd chosen to wear a dress, because she wanted this meeting to be completely opposite to their past encounters. It was soft and feminine, a nice complement to her figure. And it was very much something Katlin *Brown* would wear.

He didn't say anything.

She patted Jim for something to do. "Hello, boy," she said, and stroked his cheek.

She glanced at Quint and saw that his jaw had tightened.

"I—" she started to say and stopped. "My father told me you came to see him."

"Yes."

"He said...you wanted to see me."

Once again, he was silent.

She moved uncomfortably in the palpable tension and admitted, "I wanted to see you, too."

"Why?"

She hadn't expected such a direct question, but knew she should have. It was his way. "Because I feel bad about what happened. And about what you think of me."

"What do I think of you?"

"You made yourself pretty clear."

"Maybe I was wrong."

"You *were* wrong," she agreed quickly.

Katlin shuffled. He was so contained, so controlled! She started to doubt that she would get anywhere. She looked up…directly into the fire that had started to build in his eyes. She instinctively took a step back.

Quint, still holding Jim's reins, clasped the back of her neck with his free hand. His strong fingers tightened, pulling her close. The kiss he then gave her, half in and half out of the shade, with the horse as a silent witness, had all the pent-up longing of a love nearly lost.

When, finally, their lips parted, he said fiercely, "There. Does that tell you what I think?"

Katlin smiled unsteadily. "You—you may have to show me again sometime."

His fingers once again tightened. "Anytime," he said and gave her another long kiss.

Jim, growing impatient, shifted position and jerked his head. They were in camp. He still wore his saddle. He was tired. He was thirsty. And he wouldn't mind a snack. Somehow, he managed to get that all across to the pair who broke apart, laughing.

"Maybe I'd better take care of Jim," Quint said dryly.

"Probably a good idea," Katlin agreed.

"You'll be here when I get back?"

"Try and chase me away."

Quint held her gaze, then led the horse away.

Katlin watched them go, her optimism rising. Was it possible they would be able to work things out?

Quint came back less than five minutes later, and Katlin was exactly where he'd left her. Without a word, he walked straight up and swept her into his arms. Only this time he didn't kiss her. He held her against him, the side of her face pressed to his chest, his fingers threaded in her hair.

This had to be one of the sweetest moments of Katlin's life. His action spoke volumes, as did hers. She held him just as tightly.

"I thought I'd lost you," he said huskily.

Katlin, who just days before had felt at a loss about who she was and what she felt, was now complete in her knowledge. She whispered, "Never!"

He took her into the trailer with him, then, lifting her easily, carried her to the bedroom and placed her on the bed.

The levelheaded portion of Katlin knew they should wait. Knew that as fragile as their reconciliation was at this point, intimacy could come too soon. But as he crawled onto the bed and leaned over her, looking down with those electrically charged blue eyes—now totally alive with desire— she couldn't refuse him. Or herself.

She accepted every demand of his hands, of his mouth, loving the feel of them on her body. She reveled in touching him, appreciating the hard sculpture of his muscles, appreciating her freedom to explore. He brought her to such a state that she could barely stand to wait while they helped each other free of their remaining clothes. The further intimacy was more than he could handle and he soon pressed her back and thrust into her.

Katlin gave a little cry of pleasure, then found even more pleasure as his rhythmic movements carried her to a point where she cried out again...because this time it was more than *she* could handle. She burst into a realm of excitement and joy that she had never reached before. An experience that he, too, shared, until he collapsed, spent, at her side.

Tears of happiness gathered in Katlin's eyes.

She lay with him cradled in her arms, breathing hard, and then breathing easier as their heart rates slackened and languidness took over.

Finally, he raised his head. "That was nice," he said, smiling.

Katlin trailed her fingers through his hair. "Mmm," she murmured back, smiling as well.

He moved until he could cradle her in his arms, the top of her head tucked under his chin, her arm across his chest. His strength and his warmth enveloped her.

They lay there for a long time, enjoying the intimacy. Then Katlin, knowing the time had come, stirred and said softly, "Quint...we need to talk."

He gave her a wonderful, lazy, sexy smile. "I thought we *were* talking," he teased.

"No, 'talk'...As in, use words. Not—"

"I like the 'not.'"

"I know. I do, too. Only—"

He relented and arranged pillows so they could sit up. "I know what you mean."

"It's important that we get this straight. Everything that— What happened—" She tried again. "I never set out to make you care for me, Quint. I only wanted you to trust me, so when I told you who I was and asked about Michael, you would tell me the truth. I know I lied, but—"

He interrupted her. "I don't have a problem with that anymore."

"You did last week."

"I know. But I thought about what you said, and it made sense. Intruders on the ranch are usually met with a rifle."

"Would you have agreed to talk to me if I'd told you who I was right away?"

"Probably not," he said honestly.

"Or if I'd told you about Michael?"

"That would have been harder."

"Would I have even gotten that far?"

"We'd probably never have met. If I'd asked Mae to keep you away, she would have."

Katlin nodded. Just as she'd thought.

"Everything...got out of hand," she went on. "I wanted to tell you, but I couldn't figure out how, and the longer it took for me to do it, the worse the problem became. It reached the point where every time I told you a lie, it was like…''

He pulled her close and said huskily, ''Someday you're going to have to set me straight on a few things. I'm not sure what's real and what isn't about you. I know you didn't grow up in Lafayette.''

''No.''

There was a slight pause. ''I don't want you to go away again, Katlin.''

She kissed him in reassurance. ''I won't. Not as long as you want me with you. And I'll never tell you another lie. That's not the way I am, Quint. Not the way I was raised.''

''Sometimes a lie…isn't bad. Sometimes it's done to keep people from being hurt. That's what you did.''

''I did more than that. I told lie after lie. I got so sick of it!''

''I've lied before, Katlin.''

She looked at him. ''To me?''

''To everyone.''

She saw the look on his face that she'd seen before—the sadness, the turning inward. ''Does this have to do with…Michael?'' she asked carefully. She was afraid of what he was going to tell her. It wouldn't make a difference to the way she felt about him, but she dreaded hearing him admit that he bore responsibility for what had happened.

''I told your father part of this, and there's many

parts I can't tell you either, but—I owe you the truth you came for. Especially after everything that's happened.'' He met her gaze. ''Michael was a hero, Katlin. I was with him when he died. We were under fire. He hung out of the helicopter to help two of the wounded on board, and he was hit. Right in front of my eyes. I don't think he suffered, because it happened so fast and was so—he died almost immediately.'' He paused. ''He didn't have to put himself at risk like that. But if he hadn't, those of us on the ground might have died. We got away just in time. A few seconds later and—''

Katlin held Quint's hand, sensing his need for comfort. Having to relive what had happened was difficult for him. Moisture, again, welled in her eyes. From childhood, she'd always looked to Michael as a hero. And he'd truly been one. Then to hear that Quint had been so close to death at the same time—

''Is…what you were doing…wherever it was…part of what you can't tell me?''

''I shouldn't be telling you any of this. But yes. It is.''

She swallowed. ''What about—what about what happened after? Why you—''

He sat forward, breaking her grasp. But he quickly reached for her hand again.

''This is where the lie comes in,'' he said. He glanced at her and she saw more pain. ''I have to give you a little history here, so you'll understand.

You know my father was career Army and that he was proud to be an enlisted man—a sergeant.''

She nodded.

''He had a good friend who ended up a colonel. My father saved his life in Korea when they were both young and the colonel never let an opportunity go by to repay him. He and his wife were like family to us. He was the only officer my father could stomach.'' He explained, ''There's always this tension between enlisted men and officers. Well, my father thought the world of the colonel and the feeling was returned. They respected each other. The colonel is the reason I became an officer. He encouraged me to go to Officer Candidate School when my dad wanted me to be a non-com, like him. The colonel thought I should do more and he talked my dad around to accepting it. And when my dad got sick...the colonel watched out for him then, as well. Made sure he had good care and that my mom and sister and I could be with him when he died. The colonel was a special man, decorated, served in two wars. Highly thought of. At the time of the mission, he was also three months away from retirement...and I found out later, sick himself. Only he didn't tell anyone. I saw a sign of it when I talked to him last...but he shrugged it off.''

He looked at her again and she smiled understanding.

He went on, ''The colonel gave me my mission briefing...and he forgot to include a vital instruction, because of his illness. An instruction that caused the mission to be compromised.''

''And that caused Michael's....''

He nodded. ''When I got back to base I learned that the colonel had suffered a stroke and was in a pretty bad way. He was alive, but barely. Some months later he died without ever regaining consciousness. I was the only person who knew what the colonel had or hadn't told me that day. I couldn't let him be blamed.''

''So you took it on yourself,'' she said after a stunned moment. ''When your superiors came looking for someone to blame, you told them—''

''A lie.''

''But Quint—''

''And I'd do it again,'' he swore. ''In a heartbeat.''

Katlin gazed at him with open awe. She'd known he had strong character, but she'd never expected such a noble act! Such sacrifice.

''But what about your career?''

''It was over. I resigned my commission and left.''

''Then you came back here.''

He nodded.

Katlin absorbed everything he'd said. She wasn't sure who was holding whose hand tighter.

He spoke again. ''I thought you'd come to stir it all up again. Used me to get the story for some kind of news program. The powers that be, both in the

Army and out of it, want to forget the mission ever happened. They slapped a highly sensitive classification on it. As I told your father, I could go to jail for telling you just the little I have. But most important is the colonel's name, and that his wife, who's still alive, can carry on with her life and her good memories." He shook his head, giving a wounded smile. "Kinda put me in a pickle when you told me what the officer had implied about your brother. I couldn't let that stand. I had to set it straight. So I went to see your father."

"And he agreed to keep it quiet?"

"He's a good man. He understood. He said no purpose would be served by bringing it all up again, and that what I'd told him would stay in the family."

"He *is* a good man," Katlin said softly.

"Katlin…I barely knew your brother. We met on a plane the day of the mission. Just like I met the others."

She heard an anguished echo when he spoke of the lost men.

"It's not your fault, Quint! The men who died… none of them would blame you. Michael wouldn't. I know he wouldn't! And the colonel…if he was the kind of man you said he was, he'd be upset about what you did—taking the blame—but he'd also be proud that you're the man you are."

Quint reached into a drawer of the chest beside the bed and brought out the photo she'd left for him.

"I wish I had known him," he murmured, and handed the snapshot back to her.

Katlin bit her lip as she gazed at the familiar faces. Then she thought of her dream and her mother's. "I think Michael would want you to move on with your life, Quint. He wouldn't want you to hide yourself away. I think...I *know*...he'd think you're okay. And to him, 'okay' was as good as a person could get."

Quint smoothed a hand over her shoulder, but said nothing.

Katlin lifted the hand she had hold of and carried it to her lips. If she hadn't cared for him before, she would have now, after hearing this.

Quint was like a man from another time, where honor and courage were admired, rewarded. She admired him more than she could put into words.

She loved him.

Quint pulled her to him and held her close.

"So," he said after a moment, setting the photo on top of the chest for her. "That's kind of where we stand. On equal ground."

"What you did was more—" she started to say.

"Equal ground," he repeated.

She was silent a moment. Then, "Quint?"

"Yes?"

"Would this be a good time to tell you I love you?"

She sensed the wry smile that pulled at his lips.

But her declaration had been given with such sincerity, he must have decided not to tease her.

"Any time's a good time for that," he said softly.

"Then...I do," she affirmed.

"You don't think it's too soon?"

"No."

"Then you won't mind if I tell you the same."

"The same...what?"

He smiled fully this time. She saw it when she drew back to look at him.

"You know," he pretended to hedge.

"I'd like to hear."

He twisted around until he had her lying back on the bed and gazing into his devil blue eyes—

Hadn't she thought in the beginning that she would stand toe-to-toe with the devil himself in order to find her answer? Well, she was still looking for an answer, only this time it was a much different one. One she'd never even imagined searching for...and from a man who was anything *but* a devil.

He touched her lips softly with his. "I love you enough to have left this place and gone looking for you. I love you enough to give up this life if it's not something you want. I enjoy taking care of cattle and ranging free...but I love you more."

"You'd give up being a cowboy?"

"I gave up being a soldier."

"It's not the same."

"I liked being a soldier."

"But this—" She paused. "When I first came

here I didn't know anything about ranches. And I didn't really care. But after being with you—''

"What are you going to do now?" he asked. "What did you want to do before all this started?"

She grimaced. "Well, you know that English degree I told you about? It's really an MBA."

He whistled softly. "Then you truly can do whatever you want, where you want."

"But...I'm not sure what I *want* anymore. Except you!"

"Then stay with me."

"On the ranch?"

"For now. We have the trailer, a truck, a car and two horses."

She giggled. "What would the Parkers say? And Mae? And the Hugheses?"

"Mae'll say she planned it all along. And who knows? Maybe she did. My Uncle Dub couldn't believe she let you come stay out here in the first place. As for everyone else? Aunt Delores is already calling you my lady friend."

"She is?"

"Well, she said she was glad I had found me one."

Katlin couldn't restrain herself. She laughed joyfully until Quint put a stop to it...by pulling her back against him and giving her something else to think about.

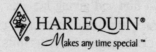

WELCOME TO

If this is your first visit to the friendly ranching town in the hill country of Texas, get ready to meet some unforgettable people. If you've been there before, you'll be happy to see some old faces and meet new ones.

Harlequin Superromance® and Margot Dalton—author of seven books in the original Crystal Creek series—are pleased to offer three **brand-new** stories set in Crystal Creek.

IN PLAIN SIGHT by **Margot Dalton**
On sale May 2000

CONSEQUENCES by **Margot Dalton**
On sale July 2000

THE NEWCOMER by **Margot Dalton**
On sale September 2000

HARLEQUIN®
Makes any time special ™

HARLEQUIN®
SUPERROMANCE®

*Pregnant and alone—
these stories follow women
from the heartache of
betrayal to finding true love
and starting a family.*

THE FOURTH CHILD by C.J. Carmichael.
When Claire's marriage is in trouble, she tries to
save it—although she's not sure she can forgive her
husband's betrayal.
On sale May 2000.

AND BABY MAKES SIX by Linda Markowiak.
Jenny suddenly finds herself jobless and pregnant by
a man who doesn't want their child.
On sale June 2000.

MOM'S THE WORD by Roz Denny Fox.
After her feckless husband steals her inheritance and
leaves town with another woman, Hayley discovers she's
pregnant.
On sale July 2000.

Available wherever Harlequin books are sold.

HARLEQUIN®
Makes any time special ™